DREAM WANDERERS
Trials

PAULA BROWN

A Mouse Gate™ Adventure

Mouse Gate™
1103 Middlecreek
Friendswood, Texas 77546
281-992-3131 TEL
www.MouseGate.com

ISBN: 978-1-59095-018-0
UPC: 6-43977-60186-5
Library of Congress Control Number:

Printed in the United States of America with simultaneous
printings in Australia, Canada, and United Kingdom.
FIRST EDITION
1   2   3   4   5   6   7   8   9   10

To Tricia and Rob,
for making my dreams come true.

A special Thank You to my sister Nancy.
This wouldn't have been possible without you.

About the Author

Paula Brown is a freelance travel writer who also has a love for science fiction and Walt Disney World. Paula is the coauthor of *Dining at Walt Disney World: The Definitive Guide*. She is also a contributing author to *InsiderScoop® to Walt Disney World®* series of books. Other works of fiction include The *Coffee Cruiser* and *It's About Time*.

Paula lives in Florida with her husband and daughter.

About the Book

Dream Wanderers guide you through your worst night-mares. Far across the universe, an elite school runs a special program, training the Dream Wanderers of tomorrow.

Prologue

Gren waited for Lawson outside of the entrance to Epcot. She had already been through security and she stood on the side. He would know where to find her. Gren had never been happier. She lived in a small apartment; it was the first time that she had ever lived on her own. Her parents helped her with the rent. She had an internship in which she was gaining valuable experience. The internship didn't pay much, so she had a part time job on the side. She also attended college online. She was busy, but somehow, she managed to keep her Mondays free. Each Monday she and Lawson would hit one of the Walt Disney World parks. Gren had an Annual Pass because her parents were Disney Vacation Club members, and she made sure that she used it. She and Lawson would also sometimes get together during the week for dinner or a movie. Things were about to change, and at the early hour she didn't want to think about it.

Lawson had quickly become Gren's best friend. She felt like she had known him for her entire life. Their feelings for each other went deeper than friendship, but they were both busy and they knew that the timing wasn't right. While Gren's parents helped her out financially and emotionally, Lawson didn't have any family because he was orphaned at an early age. He worked at a local restaurant and was putting himself through college. He also had an Annual Pass, and had been able to arrange his schedule so that he could spend Mondays in the parks with Gren.

When Gren saw Lawson walk through the security line she waved to get his attention. "Sorry I'm late," Lawson said as he approached her.

"No, I was early." They shared a hug, then proceeded towards the main entrance. Gren had something that she needed to tell Lawson, something that she knew he wouldn't be happy about, but she decided to wait until the end of the day. She wanted to have a great time with her best friend, instead of talking about what was soon going to happen. "Head right to Soarin'?" Gren asked.

"Sounds like a plan." They hurried towards the ride because they knew that the line was already forming. Since the park had just opened, they were relieved to see that the wait wasn't too long. As they stood in line, they caught each other up on the previous week's events.

"My parents might be coming for a long weekend next month," Gren said. "They're talking about reserving a room at the BoardWalk, they've never stayed there before. It would be Friday through Sunday, so we'd still have our Monday."

"Would Winnie come too?"

"Yeah, my little sister would never forgive them if they went to Disney without her." Gren paused. "I was thinking that maybe it would be a good time for you to finally meet them. We could all have dinner or something. I know that Winnie wants to see you again."

"I'd love to see her as well." Lawson paused. "Has she said anything?"

Gren shook her head. "My parents would just say that she has an active imagination. I think that she's decided that the whole thing was just a dream."

"I sometimes think that it was too," Lawson admitted. "But then I look at my 'Magical FASTPASS' and I become more confused than ever."

"Three more months," Gren mumbled.

"It was a great way to meet," Lawson said with a smile. Almost two years earlier they had met because a total stranger named Roy gave them special FASTPASSES for Rock 'n' Roller Coaster. It was a ride that they would never forget. The tickets had only the day and the month on them, and they had been able to use them again the following year. The second time Gren's sister Winnie rode with them as well.

"I haven't been able to find Winnie's pass," Gren said. "I know where mine is, but hers seems to have disappeared."

"I guess she's just not meant to ride it next time," Lawson said. He noticed that the woman with three children in line in front of them was listening to their conversation, so he decided to change the subject. "What time is our Test Track FastPass+ for?"

"10:45 until 11:45," Gren replied. "We'll make it without any problems. We should be boarding here soon."

A few minutes later Gren and Lawson were watching the video before the ride. They had seen it so many times that they could recite it word for word. They then took their seats and enjoyed one of their favorite attractions.

Once the ride was over they had some time to kill before Test Track. They rode Spaceship Earth because the line was short. After that was over they stopped to watch the Fountain of Nations, where someone caught Gren's eye. "Lawson, look," she said. "That girl over there looks a lot like Calli."

"You're right, they could be twins. Let's get a closer look, without being obvious or creepy."

The young woman looked like she was close to Gren and Lawson's age. Lawson took one step in the girl's direction and she took off. She didn't run, but she did walk quickly and headed right into a tour group that had just arrived. Lawson picked up his pace and Gren followed.

The young woman seemed to be purposely trying to keep ahead of Gren and Lawson. They didn't really know why they were trying to catch up to her. In the back of her mind Gren wondered if maybe the young woman had been through the same type of occurrence that she and Lawson had experienced twice. She didn't know how she was going to ask a total stranger if anything weird had ever happened on Rock 'n' Roller Coaster.

Lawson got ahead of Gren, and he kept his eyes on the girl. She seemed to know that they were following her. He kept glancing back to make sure that Gren was still close behind. He had to walk around a family to avoid getting in their picture, and the young woman managed to put some distance between herself and her pursuers. At one point she dropped something, but she didn't stop to pick it up. Lawson continued to follow, while Gren picked up the two small objects that were on the ground. The girl turned a corner, and suddenly she was out of sight. Lawson returned to Gren. "It's like she disappeared," he said.

"She dropped these." Gren held up the objects. "They're two of those pressed penny things. Look at where they're from."

Lawson took one of the pennies from Gren. "Test Track."

"Let's go ride," Gren suggested. "It's just about time for our FastPass+. The park isn't busy today, there's a good chance that we'll see her again."

"You're right," Lawson agreed. "Let's go."

Gren and Lawson had a good time designing their own concept car for the ride. They always took turns on the design choices and they tried to make the car as outrageous as possible. Gren used her phone to take a picture of the final design. She did it each time that they rode Test Track.

A few minutes later a cast member instructed them to get into the first row. That was good, they preferred the front to the back. Gren glanced at the Single Rider Line to see who would be paired with them. She noticed that the girl who looked like Calli was in the line. As she was about to point her out to Lawson, they were told to board.

After Gren fastened her seat belt she took another glance at the Single Rider Line. The young woman was no longer there, meaning that she had been given a ride assignment; or that she had never really been there at all. As Gren turned her head back around she noticed that a teenage boy had been placed in the row that she and Lawson were in. He was holding a baseball hat in his hands. Behind them sat a mother with a nervous daughter. A single rider had been placed in the row with them...it was the girl who looked like Calli.

Gren reached into her pocket and pulled out one of the two pressed pennies. Lawson still had the other one. She turned around. "Here," she said to the young woman, "I think you dropped this earlier." Gren's voice caused Lawson to look and he was surprised to see Calli's doppelganger.

"Thanks, but keep it," the woman said. "I have another one."

The ride started to move forward. "She sounds just like her," Lawson whispered to Gren. "Maybe since we're in the same car we'll be able to talk to her after the ride is over."

"Yeah," Gren whispered back, "but what would we say? You look just like someone who we know from a parallel universe?"

"Good point."

They sat back because the ride had started. Gren could not stop thinking about the young woman seated behind them. The news that she had to share with Lawson also weighed heavily on her mind. Her favorite part of the ride was the end, when it looked like they were about to hit a wall but instead the car went outside and sped up to 65MPH. Gren sat back to enjoy it. As they neared the fake wall, everything started to blur.

The Learning Center's Covenant

As a Dream Wandering student at the Learning Center, I promise to take my gift seriously. I will use this gift only within the laws and regulations of Terra. I will spend time with my partner, knowing that this relationship is vital to my completion of the program. I will have no physical contact with students of the opposite gender. I will follow the rules of the Learning Center, knowing that those in charge know what is best for me.

Signature _____

Date _____

Chapter One

There was a loud clap of thunder. "I'm scared." A boy of about five sat in a corner by himself. He was visibly shaking. "The thunder is going to get me."

"There's no reason to be afraid." Gren's voice was smooth and calming. "Thunder is just a noise, it can't hurt you."

"But the lightning that causes it can," the boy argued, his voice trembling. "Lightning hit our house an orbit ago and it burned to the ground."

Gren suddenly realized why the boy was so afraid, and was a little bit upset that an important piece of information had been withheld from her. "The chances of that happening again are so low that it's almost impossible. Remember that thunder is just a noise. Now look around the room. What is here that can help keep you safe?"

The boy looked up and pointed towards the ceiling. "We have an alarm in the new house so that we'll know if there is another fire."

"That's good, your parents are working hard to keep you safe." Gren purposely repeated the word. She could tell that safety was something that the child sought. "What else have they done?"

The boy glanced around again. "We have anti-fire devices in each room. If there is another fire, we can put it out quickly."

"Is that all that your parents have done?"

"No. We have a plan now. If there is another fire, my sister and I know all of the different ways that we can get out. I even have a ladder in my room that I can throw out the window. We're all supposed to meet in our neighbor's yard if there is another fire."

"See," Gren's voice said, "your parents have it under control. They know what needs to be done if there is another emergency, and they are looking out for you and your sister. You're much safer now."

"I guess." There was another clap of thunder, but the boy didn't flinch quite as much.

"The thunder is just a sound. A sound can't hurt you."

"Okay," the boy said at last. "I'll try to be brave."

"You are brave," Gren's voice informed him. "You don't need to try." Everything went black.

∘ ∘ ⦿ ◯ ∘ ∘

A few hundreds later Gren was seated in Haas' office. "Not bad. It's going to take a few more sessions with him, but you've started to help him to get over his fear. Nice touch, the part about him being brave. You were able to help him to reach inside of himself there."

"Sir," Gren said slowly, "why wasn't I told that his house was destroyed in a fire? Wasn't that an important piece of information for a Wanderer to know?"

"I wanted to see how much you'd be able to find out," Haas explained. "Often important pieces of information are held back, and you'll find them out through wandering. Some clients don't know the source of their fears, and it's our obligation to help them dig deep down and discover that source. But you're right, I did leave out information with this child because I wanted to see how long it would take for you to find it out on your own. You and Lawson have your Clinical Trials coming up, I need to make sure that you are prepared. Speaking of Lawson...he has a session in about five hundreds. I have to observe. Quite honestly, Gren, I'm going to be so relieved once you and Lawson are finally licensed. I'll have time to concentrate on my own clients once again..."

Gren left the room and went to add her notes into the boy's file. There was a time when she would have taken Haas' last comment as an insult, but she finally realized that he only said it because he wanted her to become the best Dream Wanderer possible.

A few units later Gren and Lawson walked home together. In many ways it had become routine. They held hands, even though they couldn't officially call themselves a couple. Haas forbid inter-office dating. Once they received their licenses they had a lot that they would need to sort through, but until then, they would continue to only hold hands and be the closest friends possible.

"What do you think we can expect for the Trials?" Lawson asked. It was a conversation that they had almost every rotation.

"I have no idea," Gren replied. "I'm happy we still have some time until we have to face them. I used to hate the simulator, but now I'm glad for all the time that I have in front of it."

"Did you wander any real dreams this rotation?"

"Yeah, one." Gren was not allowed to discuss the session, it was against their oath. "Haas even almost paid me a compliment. How about you?"

Lawson looked away, not wanting to see Gren's reaction. "Um, I wandered three."

Gren pulled her hand away and stopped walking. "Three! How am I ever going to be prepared for the Trials if I get stuck in front of the stupid simulator all the time? I need to practice on real dreams! Why did he give you three clients and only give one to me? Haas obviously doesn't have any confidence in me!"

"It's not how it sounds," Lawson said. "Two of them were kids that I had wandered before. Their parents asked for me."

"You have people asking for you?"

Lawson wasn't sure how to reply. "Just a few," he said at last.

Gren walked for several micros in silence. "I'm sorry," she said. "I overreacted. It's just that I can't think about anything but the Trials. This is what I've worked for my entire life."

Lawson put his arm around Gren's shoulder. "And you'll pass. We both will. And then we'll become the best Dream Wanderers in the business."

"Yeah, sure." Gren wished that she had Lawson's confidence.

• ◦ ● ● ◦ •

A few hundreds later they stood in front of Gren's building. "You want to get together tonight?" Lawson asked. "Sham and Titus remarked this morning that it's been forever since you've been over."

"No, I just want to stay in and study. See if I can find out anything more about what to expect for the Trials."

"We need to study too," Lawson said.

"Okay, you three do that," Gren said, purposely taking Lawson's comment a way that he had not meant it. "I'll see you in the morning." Gren walked away and entered her building before Lawson had a chance to reply.

"I meant that we could all study together," Lawson said to the air.

Chapter Two

Once again, Gren poured over a book. She flipped through the pages, desperate to find some information. She had been trying to find out anything that she could about the Trials, but no one gave a hint as to what they could be about. She couldn't even find out if the Trials were an intellectual test or if instead she would be expected to do some major wandering. Her entire life had led up to the Trials, and her future depended on passing them.

"The future," Gren said aloud. That held its own set of trials. If she passed and became licensed she realized that her life was going to get a lot more complicated. She knew that she would legally be able to start practicing, but where? If she stayed in the practice that Haas owned she would make decent money. There was a lot of prestige that came with working for the best Dream Wanderer in the business. She complained about him a lot, but deep down she liked and respected the man. He was always hard on her, but she finally realized that it was because he was the best and he expected his people to be the best as well. She and Lawson were the first Apprentices that he had taken on in over two decades. If he offered her a position as an Associate Wanderer, it would be hard to turn it down.

She also thought about what becoming licensed meant for her relationship with Lawson. They were partnered together as Whites at the Learning Center, and they had been inseparable ever since. They had feelings for each other, but there had always been rules that forbade them to act on those feelings. In some ways, Gren was perfectly fine with the status quo. She liked the lines that they couldn't cross. She knew that Lawson did not feel the same way. Lawson had been her best friend since the micro that they met, and she worried about what might happen if their relationship were to change. She also knew that once the lines were gone, change was inevitable.

"Concentrate, Gren." She looked back down at the book in front of her. "There's got to be something on the Trials in here somewhere." She turned a page, aware deep down that she was looking for information that did not exist.

· ○ ○◐○ ○ ·

Lawson sat in his dwelling with his two roommates. The three of them had shared a room back at the Learning Center, and when they became Apprentices in the same city they decided to find a place together. Sham and Titus apprenticed at a different practice.

"So, what have you guys been doing to prepare for the Trials?" Lawson asked.

Sham laughed. "Prepare? Cassidy says that if we're not ready for the Trials by now, we never will be."

"I wish that Gren had that same mindset," Lawson said. "She's going to drive herself insane. I've never seen her so worried."

"Seriously?" Sham laughed again. "Gren worries about everything."

"I'm a little bit nervous about the Trials myself," Titus said quickly, hoping to stop an argument before it started. "After all, this is what we've been working for ever since we were kids."

"Are you sure that it's the Trials that Gren is worried about, and not what comes after?" Sham asked.

Lawson looked confused. "What do you mean?"

"Aw, come on, Lawson, everyone knows about your feelings for her. Maybe Gren is worried about what is going to happen with the two of you once the rules have finally been removed. Maybe she doesn't want things to change."

Lawson sat there for a micro, stunned. He had always assumed that he and Gren would finally be together once they were licensed. "We've, well, we've got a lot that we'll need to figure out."

"You don't have to do that right now," Titus quickly added. "You're right, we need to focus on the Trials."

"Have you been able to find out anything from Grey?" Lawson asked.

Sham grunted, disgusted by the name. "Grey won't tell me anything."

"All he's said to me," Titus added, "was that Cassidy made sure that he was ready. Nothing else."

"Like I'm going to base my entire future on something that Grey says anyway..."

Lawson laughed. "Sham, you always sound so jealous when Grey is mentioned!"

"Jealous! I..." He couldn't think of a good reply.

Sham and Titus apprenticed at the same practice where Grey worked. He was an orbit older, and after he passed the Trials he became one of Cassidy's Associate Wanderers. Sham and Grey barely tolerated each other, while Grey and Titus had become friends.

"No one is going to tell us anything," Titus reminded his friends. "It's not allowed."

"So, have you given any thought about what you plan to do after you're licensed?" Lawson asked.

"Are you kidding?" Sham answered quickly. "I'm not thinking about anything but the Trials!"

"So, you are worried about them," Lawson teased.

"I don't know," Sham conceded, "maybe just a little bit."

Chapter Three

"Apprentices, both of you, in my office, now." Gren and Lawson stared at each other. The tone of Haas' voice worried them. "Now! I'll be there in a micro."

"Yes, Sir," they replied in unison. Neither said another word until they were seated in the office.

"What do you think we did wrong?" Lawson whispered.

"I have no idea," Gren whispered back. "I feel like I did when we'd get sent to Ladinda's office back at the Learning Center."

There was a short laugh behind them. Haas had entered the room unnoticed. "Funny you'd mention the Learning Center. That's what I need to talk to you about. Relax, you're not in trouble."

"What about the Learning Center, Sir?" Gren asked. It was one of her favorite places on Terra.

"I received a personal request from Ladinda this morning. She asked if she could borrow both of you for a few rotations. You know me, I can't turn that woman down. If I could, I never would have ended up with...anyway, she has a project and said that she needs you both to help her with it."

"A project? What kind of project?" Lawson asked.

"That's all that she told me. You leave the rotation after next. I have no idea how long you'll be gone, but she did promise that you'll be able to practice. And since we're working on the payback percentage system, you'll be paid while you're gone. Until then, it's business as usual around here." Haas pointed towards the door and the two Apprentices stood up. "Gren, you have a session in a unit, Lawson, your first session of the rotation is in ten hundreds, so you need to get ready. You've wandered this client before. Aribella will be observing this time, I do have my own clients that I need to take care of." Haas motioned towards the door again and Gren and Lawson left the office. As Haas closed the door behind them he could be heard saying to himself, "I can't wait until the Trials are over and things return to normal around here. I never would have accepted Apprentices if it hadn't been a personal request from Ladinda..."

Since Lawson had to prepare for a session, he and Gren did not have time to talk about what Ladinda might want them for. It ended up being a busy rotation. Since she was going to be gone for an undisclosed amount of time, Gren wanted to practice in front of the simulator as much as possible. She also had a strong session with the one client that she wandered. A small part of her felt prepared for the Trials, but the rest of her was terrified. At the end of the rotation she looked for her best friend. It was usually the other way around, Lawson would have to find her.

"You ready to go?" Gren asked. Lawson nodded. He was slightly nervous that Gren would ask how many children he had wandered. It had been a busy rotation for him, he had wandered four times. "Good. Let's get out of here." Gren waited until they were outside before asking the question that had been on her mind the entire rotation. "What do you think Ladinda wants us for?"

"I have no idea."

"Oh, Lawson, I can't wait to be back at the Learning Center for a few rotations. We've only been back twice since we left, and once was for Calli and Tayo's graduation so we didn't even get to talk to everyone. Spending a few rotations there is going to be great!"

"Want to come over?" Lawson asked. "Then we can brag to Sham and Titus that we're getting a paid vacation and they're not."

"It's not a vacation and we do have to payback a good amount of what we're earning...but sure." They walked past Gren's building and continued down the street. "I wonder what Ladinda wants."

"Maybe it has something to do with a male/female partnering. We are, after all, the only ones to make it all the way through the program."

"Remember Angel and Dod? They'd be..." Gren thought for a micro, "...Purples this unit."

"If they're still in the program. A lot of kids don't make it, and Dod did have a problem with the fact that Angel is a girl."

"They'll make it," Gren said. She took Lawson's hand. He was surprised, it was usually the other way around. "We proved that it can be done."

The rest of the walk to Lawson's dwelling they talked about Ladinda's mysterious project and reminisced about their rotations at the Learning Center. They arrived at the building and Lawson pulled out his key. "They're going to be surprised to see you," he said, referring to his roommates. "It has been a while." He opened the door and saw immediately that the place was a mess. "Holy spl..." Lawson stopped mid-word. Gren was standing next to him and he knew how much she hated a certain expression. "...glidemobile, what's going on?"

"Holy glidemobile?" Gren whispered to her best friend.

"Hey Lawson!" Sham replied. "Gren! Sorry about the mess. Good to see you. It's been too long."

"What's going on?" Lawson repeated.

"We're packing," Sham explained.

"Packing? What for?"

Titus came in from a back room. "Gren! Good to see you. It's been too long."

"Packing?" Lawson repeated. "Where are you going?"

Sham and Titus exchanged a glance. They knew that Gren was feeling stressed over the Trials, and weren't sure how she would take the news. Sham finally answered. "Ladinda wants us to help with something at the Learning Center for a few rotations."

Lawson and Gren both grinned. "Great," Lawson said. "You can give us a ride. She wants us there too. I thought we were going to have to take public transportation."

Chapter Four

Both Gren and Lawson realized that Haas would not give them any information on the mysterious trip to the Learning Center, so Sham and Titus decided to see if they could learn anything from Cassidy. They left for work a few hundreds early so that they could talk to her. When they arrived, Titus knocked on the office door.

"Come in." Titus and Sham entered the office. Even though Cassidy often claimed that she was going to clean off her desk, it was more of a mess than ever. "You two are here early. Sham, you have the first session this morning, Titus you'll observe. Then you'll switch. It's going to be a busy rotation, I had to rearrange some things because of your surprise exit. I'm glad you came in early, that shows me that you're both being responsible and thinking about the practice. Now, if you'll excuse me..."

Sham realized that they had just received a compliment that they did not deserve. "Um, about our 'surprise exit', as you called it. Did Ladinda give you any more information?"

"I told you everything that she said to me. You know Ladinda, she does what she wants, when she wants, and she can get away with it because, well, because she's Ladinda."

"Gren and Lawson are going also," Titus added.

"Hmmm. Interesting. Okay, boys, it's time to start the rotation. If you see Grey will you send him in here? I need to go over his new workload with him. He'll have to pick up some extra sessions while you're gone. I just wish that I knew how long it was going to be for."

"Us too," Sham said. He and Titus left the office. "That wasn't very helpful."

"Did you feel as bad as I did when she thought that we came in early because we were being responsible?"

"Yeah." Sham laughed. "She should know us better than that by now."

"Let's go look for Grey," Titus suggested. "We only have a few hundreds until the first session, and Cassidy said that she needs to talk to him."

"Look for Grey," Sham repeated. "Three of my favorite words."

* * * * * * *

After checking everywhere, Titus and Sham realized that Grey hadn't yet arrived for work. They waited by the front door. "Hey Grey," Titus called out as soon as he entered, "Cassidy needs to see you."

"I wonder why," Grey replied.

"You're probably in trouble," Sham quickly jumped in. "Maybe she found out about that thing that you did. You know the one I'm talking about." Sham didn't know of anything that Grey had done wrong, he just liked antagonizing him.

"Ignore him," Titus said. "Sham and I are heading to the Learning Center for a few rotations, so Cassidy needs to go over the new schedule with you. That's all."

"Why are you heading to the Learning Center?"

"It's a personal invitation from Ladinda," Sham bragged. "She wanted us, not you."

"Ignore him," Titus repeated. "I'm not sure what it's about, supposedly Ladinda has a project that she needs our help with. Gren and Lawson are going too."

"Have a good time," Grey said. "I haven't been to the Learning Center since Tayo graduated."

"Calli graduated that rotation as well," Sham said quickly. "Ignore him."

Grey grinned. "Titus, I always do."

It was a long rotation at work. When it was finally over, Sham and Titus climbed into Sham's glidemobile. They lived close enough so that they could walk, but Sham was happy that he finally owned a vehicle, so they usually rode. "Maybe while we're there we can go visit Roy," Sham said. "It's been a long time since I've seen him."

"Let's see what Ladinda wants first," Titus said. "Knowing her, this isn't going to be a vacation."

"You think Gren is going to be at our place when we get home?"

Titus thought for only a micro. "Definitely. She's going to want to know if Cassidy told us anything."

Sure enough, Gren was waiting at the dwelling as Sham and Titus arrived at their place. "Did you find anything out?" she asked immediately.

"Hello, Gren," Sham replied sweetly. "It's nice to see you too."

"Ignore him," Titus said. "If Cassidy does know anything about why Ladinda wants us there, she wouldn't tell us. She did complain a lot about the extra work that our absence is going to cause."

"Grey complained about it too," Sham added with a grin.

"Food!" Lawson called. He was in the back of the dwelling, preparing the evening meal. "We can talk about this while we eat."

After they ate the four friends relaxed for a while. Lawson was grateful for the upcoming trip. Gren seemed to be stressing a little less over the upcoming Trials. She was a bit worried about why they were being summoned to the Learning Center, but that was better than the stress that she had been placing on herself about the future. It was good to see her almost relax. Lawson knew how much Gren loved the Learning Center, so going back for a few rotations would do her some good.

"Maybe Ladinda will give us a hint about the Trials," Sham said. Lawson shot him a dirty look. It was the first time that the Trials had been mentioned all evening.

Gren shook her head. "She won't give anything away. It's against the rules to tell Apprentices about the Trials."

"You know Ladinda and her rules," Lawson added. One rule at the Learning Center was that students were not allowed to have any physical contact with students of the opposite gender. It was a rule that he had struggled with his entire time there. He had hated that he couldn't give Gren a hug when something good happened, or place a hand on her shoulder when she needed to be comforted. Gren had accepted the rule more easily than he had.

"So, will you two follow the 'no contact' rule once again while we're there?" Sham teased. "You know, for old time's sake."

Lawson put his arm around Gren's shoulder and pulled her close. "Nope."

Chapter Five

Gren kept looking out her window. She could not remember the last time that she had been so excited. She had no idea how long they would be at the Learning Center, but she knew that it would not be long enough. Even though she had grown used to her life in the city, she thought that the Learning Center would always feel like home. In many ways, it was more home to her than the house that her parents and little sister Winnie lived in.

The glidemobile had barely slowed down when Gren grabbed her bag and ran outside. "What took you so long?" she asked the micro that a door opened. She wasn't asking anyone in particular, just whoever had opened the door.

"We're early!" Sham exclaimed. He opened the luggage compartment and Gren threw her bag in.

"Not early enough," Gren teased. "I've been ready for over a unit."

"Of course, you have," Sham replied before they both got into the glidemobile.

It took a little over two units to get to the Learning Center. At first they talked about what Ladinda might want. They then reminisced about their orbits there, especially their final orbit. It was obvious that all four friends were excited to be returning for a few rotations. Once they arrived, Sham found a spot to park and they all got out. They decided to leave their things in the glidemobile until after their meeting with Ladinda.

As they walked towards her office, a group of Whites ran by. "It seems strange to think that those kids hadn't even taken their placement exams yet when we were here," Gren commented.

"Even stranger to think that someone else has our room," Sham added.

"Life goes on," Titus said.

Lawson was quiet. He wanted more than anything to take Gren's hand, but he knew that she would pull away. The path to Ladinda's office was one that they knew all too well. They had made the trip countless times, especially during their final orbit.

Once they arrived at the correct building, the group stopped and stared at it for a few micros. "Why do I feel like we're in trouble?" Sham asked.

"Because that was the only reason we were ever sent to see Ladinda," Titus replied.

"Let's find out what's going on," Gren suggested. She was the first one to take a step towards the building.

Once they reached Ladinda's office they paused again. None of the three guys seemed to want to knock. Finally, Gren rolled her eyes and did it herself. "Come in," a voice said sweetly from the other side.

Ladinda looked exactly the same. She smiled and gave each of her former students a hug. She then took her seat behind her desk, and motioned for them to sit down as well. "You all look so professional!" she exclaimed. "I know that I saw you at last orbit's graduation, but we didn't really have a chance to catch up. Sham, Titus, you're still apprenticing with Cassidy, right?" They both nodded. "How is that going?"

"Cassidy is the best," Titus said. Sham continued to nod in agreement.

"And how about Haas?" Ladinda asked. "Is he still giving you a hard time?"

Gren thought for a micro to find the right words. "He's making sure that we're prepared for the Trials."

Ladinda laughed. "The Trials. Don't worry about the Trials, Gren, you'll do fine. Have you given any thought to what you plan to do after you're licensed?"

Gren shook her head. "Not much. I'm focusing more on the Trials than on anything else right now."

Ladinda leaned forward and looked directly at Gren. "Don't stress about the Trials. If there is anyone who will fly through them, Gren, it's you." She leaned back again. "How about the rest of you. What might your futures hold?"

"Cassidy said that we can stay with her if we want to," Titus said. "Neither of us have decided whether or not we're going to take her up on that, but the offer is out there."

"How about you, Lawson?"

"I'm...um...I'm concentrating mostly on helping Gren get ready for the Trials." Gren shot him a dirty look.

Ladinda smiled. "I'm not surprised." She took a deep breath. "You're probably wondering why I asked you to come here. Well, I can't tell you now because not everyone has arrived yet. You'll understand soon enough." She reached into her desk drawer and pulled out some keys. "Here, you'll be staying in the Teachers' Building, at least for now. The room numbers are on the keys. Why don't you go and get settled? Grab something to eat as well. Then meet me back here in, say, four units." Ladinda stood up.

All four former students knew that once Ladinda stood up, it was time to leave. They each took a key and thanked her. Ladinda showed them out of her office.

● ○ ○◉○ ○ ●

None of the Apprentices had ever been in the Teachers' Building before. They felt as if they were intruding somehow. Lawson, Sham, and Titus found their room on the first floor. Gren's room was on the second floor. She noticed right away that it was set for three people, not just one.

After they had put away their things they met up and headed to the dining area. Everything felt so strange. They had eaten there three times a rotation for orbits, but suddenly they did not feel like they belonged. After the meal they wandered around the campus, killing time. They ended up by the lake, which did not surprise any of them.

"So, what's your room like?" Titus asked Gren.

"It's a lot bigger than the old dorms. It's setup for three people, not just me."

"Ladinda did say that not everyone was here yet," Lawson commented. He glanced around the lake and memories came flooding back to him. He and Gren had spent countless units there when they were in school.

"That's probably it," Gren agreed. "I hope I don't get stuck with two people who I can't get along with."

"Or who can't get along with each other," Sham added. "Remember how much Calli and Tayo used to fight? And you were always caught in the middle of it."

"Yeah, but they got over that," Gren reminded him. "Now they're as close as can be."

"We might not be staying in the Teachers' Building for too

long," Lawson commented. "Ladinda said that we'll be staying there, 'at least for now'." He made quotation marks with his fingers. "I wonder what she meant by that."

"I don't know," Sham replied. "I thought that she was trying to be mysterious. Ladinda is good at that."

"Isn't it about time that we meet with her again?" Titus asked. They still had a few hundreds, but they were all curious as to what was going on. Together, they headed back to Ladinda's office.

Gren only knocked once before Ladinda's office door flew open. "Gren!" two female voices shrieked.

"Calli! Tayo!" Gren threw her arms around her former roommates. Suddenly she understood why there were two extra beds in her room.

Chapter Six

Ladinda gave the group a few hundreds to catch up. Once the hugs and the chatter died down, she motioned for everyone to take a seat. "I was hoping that this would be a nice surprise." She handed keys to Calli and Tayo. "You'll be staying in the same room as Gren. It's just like old times. Now, I'm sure you're all wondering why I brought you here. Who remembers the speech that I give at every Partnering Ceremony?"

Gren and Lawson exchanged glances. It was a speech that they knew very well. Gren started, "'This rotation you're starting on a journey.'"

Lawson decided to join her. "'A journey that will be filled with many trials, tests, and tribulations, but a journey that is indeed worth taking.'"

Ladinda smiled. "That's it. Well, there are two Purples this orbit who need to be reminded of how incredible the journey can be. Gren and Lawson, you might remember them. Angel and Dod?"

Gren nodded. "We were recently talking about them. We were wondering how they're doing."

"Unfortunately, not all that well. They're having some problems, they don't seem to understand how special a boy/girl partnering can be. I thought that with the right..." Ladinda searched for the perfect word, "...guidance that they might start to take things more seriously. They are both extremely promising students and I would hate to have to break them up or expel them, but I won't hesitate to if I need to."

"What do you want us to do, Ma'am?" Gren asked.

"Help me to set them back on the right path for their journey."

Lawson shot Gren another glance. Ladinda was as vague as ever. "How?"

Ladinda stood up. "Tell you what. I'll fill all of you in tomorrow morning. Why don't you show Calli and Tayo where you're staying? Enjoy the rest of the rotation and catch up with each other. Tomorrow, we'll get to work." She motioned towards the door. "Stop by after the morning meal and we'll go over the details."

The group all headed towards the door and walked through it. "Ladinda, Ma'am..." Gren turned back around to ask a question, but the door had already been closed behind them.

After leaving the office the friends went back to the Teachers' Building so that Calli and Tayo could drop off their things. They wanted to talk but did not feel comfortable doing it in there, so they went for a walk. They ended up once again by the lake.

"I don't know," Sham said as they all sat down near the tree. "It's weird being in the Teachers' Building. It kind of gives me the creeps."

"I like it," Gren said. "We finally get to see how the other half lives."

"You would like it," Sham said. He realized that his comment could be taken the wrong way. "Because you were always the most academic out of any of us."

Calli purposely sat as far away from Sham as possible. Whenever they saw each other he would randomly start to poke her. If they were to get into a poke war, she wanted to be the one to start it. "Who are Angel and Dod?" she asked. "The names sound vaguely familiar, but I can't place them."

"They're another boy/girl partnering," Lawson explained. "They were Whites our last orbit here. Gren and I did some work with them. Good kids."

"They're an orbit older than Winnie," Gren added. She knew how much her friends liked her little sister.

"I wonder what we're going to have to do to the poor kids," Sham said.

"Ladinda didn't say that we'd be doing anything to them," Gren said. "In fact, she didn't say much at all."

Sham grinned. "That's Ladinda. Vague as always."

The six friends sat by the lake for units. When the sun began to go down they decided to get something to eat. As they stood up Tayo made her way next to Titus. "So," she started, keeping her voice down, "how's Grey?" She hoped that Sham wouldn't hear.

"He's doing pretty well," Titus answered. "Cassidy is happy with his work, and he's been a lot easier to get along with than he was when we first started our apprenticeship."

Sham, who was ahead of them, turned around. "Are you talking about Grey? Tayo, what is going on with the two of you?"

"We're, well, we're friends."

"Grey has acquaintances, not friends."

"I consider Grey a friend," Titus said quickly.

"I do too," Gren and Lawson said in unison.

"Grey's a nice guy," Calli added.

"Honestly, Sham," Tayo scolded, "if you'd just give him a chance!"

"I..."

Calli saw her opportunity. She snuck up behind Sham. "Poke." She quickly ran away.

Everyone but Sham laughed. It felt like old times. Sham stared at Calli. "You do realize that you just declared war."

Calli smiled sweetly. "Bring it on."

Chapter Seven

The next morning they ate in the dining area once again. Gren noticed that Angel was sitting with a group of Purple girls. She pointed her out to her friends. "She's grown."

"I wonder where Dod is," Lawson commented. He and Gren looked around and neither of them saw him. No one else in the group was sure what Dod looked like. When they didn't see him after a few micros, they turned back to their food.

"I think I can see part of the problem," Gren said. "Angel and Dod aren't even eating together. To really make a partnering work, you need to spend as much free time together as possible."

"I don't know," Sham mumbled. He had just taken a bite of food so he swallowed quickly. "You're jumping to conclusions. You and Lawson were together a lot, but there were plenty of meals that you ate without him. It might be a timing thing. Just because they're not together right now doesn't mean that they aren't spending any time together."

"Good point," Gren agreed, surprised that she had said those words to Sham. "I guess we'll find out soon enough."

The conversation turned once again to their orbits at the Learning Center. It was obvious that Gren missed it the most, but they all were happy to be back. As they finished their meal Calli noticed that Angel was done as well. The young girl put away her tray and left the room. Less than a hundred later Dod walked in. Gren pointed him out. The boy glanced around, then went to get his own food. He sat down at a table by himself.

"That doesn't look good," Lawson observed. "I think he was waiting for Angel to leave."

"Let's go meet with Ladinda," Gren suggested. "She's expecting us about now. I can't wait to find out what she needs us to do." She picked up her tray and her friends followed suit. It still was second nature to all of them. They glanced back at Dod one more time, then left for their meeting.

Once they arrived at her office and took their seats Ladinda got right to business. "Angel and Dod need to start working together," she explained. "They do well enough in their sessions, but it's the interaction outside of the classroom that worries me. I want all of you to spend some time with them, let them know how important it is to be friends with your partner. Gren, Lawson, you can help them to see how special a boy/girl partnering can be. Calli and Tayo, I also want you to teach them from experience, since you two didn't always get along so well. If the four of you can show them how important it is to work together, then maybe they won't have to be separated. I think that these two Purples have great potential, and I want them to see that themselves."

Sham and Titus glanced at each other. They hadn't been mentioned. "Um, Ma'am," Sham started, "what do you want Titus and me to do?"

Ladinda smiled. "I thought that having the two of you here would be a nice balance. I didn't want Dod to think that we were teaming up against him, with all the females here. So, I don't have anything specific that I need for you to do, except to just be there and befriend the boy." She lowered her voice. "You can teach Dod that girls really aren't all that bad. Now," she continued in her normal tone, "since I have the authority, I am giving you permission to wander while you are taking care of this. As you know, the parents have all given permission already in order for their children to be here, and I pass that permission onto you. I've arranged for you to meet with the two Purples in a little over a unit. They'll be in Hutch's classroom. I trust that you remember where it is?" The six former students nodded. "Good. Hutch will fill you in a little bit more. He'll be happy to see you." Ladinda stood and motioned to the door. "Thanks again for helping. Titus, can you stay for a hundred? There's something that I want you to give to Cassidy when you return, and I don't want to forget about it."

"Do you want me to stay as well?" Sham asked.

"That's not necessary, Sham. I wouldn't want to keep you and Calli from your poke war."

Sham waited until they were out of the office and the door was closed behind them. "How did she know about that?"

Lawson laughed. "Don't you realize by now that Ladinda knows everything?"

Chapter Eight

Half a unit later Titus finally arrived at the room where he was staying with Lawson and Sham. He had a book in his hand. "Ladinda wants me to give this to Cassidy," he explained. "It's about Premonition Dreaming. She thought that Cassidy might be interested. I think that the two of them talked a bit about the concept after our adventure with Winnie and Mollie last orbit."

"Most Wanderers don't think that Premonition Dreaming is possible," Lawson commented. "Haas knows bits and pieces about what happened last orbit, and he still told Gren and me that it doesn't happen."

"Yeah, well, we know better," Titus said. "Cassidy does too. Ladinda is also open to any ideas when it comes to wandering, so it doesn't surprise me that Cassidy went to her."

"Don't care," Sham said. "What I do want to know is why it took you so long to get back here. It doesn't take half a unit to give someone a book."

Titus glanced at Lawson. "Ladinda is worried about Gren. She thinks that she's putting too much pressure on herself because of the Trials. She wanted to know how she's really doing, and figured that Lawson wouldn't give her a straight answer."

"Hey!"

"She's right," Sham agreed. "You're never objective when it comes to Gren. You'll always defend her, no matter what."

"That's because..." Lawson couldn't come up with a good reply.

"Because of the way that you feel about her," Sham finished.

"Speaking of Gren," Titus said, purposely trying to move on, "aren't we supposed to be meeting with the girls about now?"

"Yeah," Lawson said. "Let's get going."

∘ ∘ ○●○ ∘ ∘

Gren, Calli, and Tayo were waiting for their friends in the lobby of the Teachers' Building. "We need to get going," Gren said, obviously excited. She had a lot of respect for Hutch and couldn't wait to see him again. "What took you so long?"

"Titus just got back from talking to Ladinda," Sham said. He immediately realized that he shouldn't have said it.

"You were there that long?" Gren asked.

"Yeah. She gave me a book for Cassidy." He decided not to tell Gren what it was about. The last thing that she needed was to think about what had happened to her little sister and Winnie's roommate an orbit earlier. Gren was under enough stress as it was. "We talked a little bit about the future. It's really weird, speaking to Ladinda like an adult. I'm used to her being an authority figure."

Sham laughed. "Yeah, it's hard to think of her as a human being." He took a step so that he was next to Calli. "Poke."

Lawson grinned. "Yeah, Sham, you're acting like an adult now. Let's get going."

∘ ∘ ○●○ ∘ ∘

The reunion with Hutch went exactly as Gren had pictured it. There were hugs and then a lot of questions to help catch up. The classroom hadn't changed. Hutch's desk was in the front. There were a few chairs, but Hutch didn't teach a traditional academic class. His class was practical, the students got to wander. The wandering table sat in the middle of the room.

Lawson looked at the table. "I still hate that thing," he mumbled to himself.

Hutch obviously heard what Lawson had said. "The wandering table is essential to our profession."

"I don't hate all wandering tables," Lawson explained. "Just that one." He knew that Hutch understood.

Gren also understood. She decided that changing the subject was a good idea. "So, Hutch, Sir, what is it that we're here for? Ladinda mentioned Angel and Dod."

Hutch took a seat in one of the chairs instead of behind his desk. The rest of the group also sat down. "Gren, you don't need to call me 'Sir'. I'm not your teacher anymore. And yes, this is about Angel and Dod. They're struggling. I don't usually deal much with Purples but I've known these two since they were Whites. We don't want to break up the partnership, but they're not moving ahead because of their differences. Ladinda and I agree that they need to see that a male/female partnering can be something special. Like you and Lawson, I know that firsthand from when I was here. We didn't make it all the way through the program, but I was partnered with a female for a while." The six friends all nodded, they had met Hutch's former partner two orbits earlier. She hadn't become a Wanderer, so the gift of wandering had been removed. "If we have to break up Angel and Dod we will, but there are no other Purples who are even slightly struggling at the micro, so that would put them even further behind. We also don't want to expel either of them for not trying, but we will if we have to. It was Ladinda's idea to bring all six of you here. She thought that you could help."

"How?" Calli asked. She was sitting as far away from Sham as possible.

"Hang out with them," Hutch said. "All of you, as a group. Dod seems to have a problem with the fact that Angel is female, and Angel only wants to spend time with other girls. Show them that boys and girls can be friends. Good friends. Ladinda and I have arranged a few outings so that you can all get away from here for a few units each rotation. I think that having Angel and Dod spend some time with the six of you, away from the other Purples, will really help."

"Or scare them," Sham mumbled quietly.

Hutch grinned. "Try not to do that." There was a knock on the closed classroom door. "Come in."

Angel and Dod, dressed in purple uniforms, entered the room. They stood far away from each other. "You wanted to see us, Sir?" Angel said.

Hutch motioned for them to walk all the way in. "Angel, Dod, you remember Gren and Lawson, don't you? From when you were Whites." They both nodded. "These are their friends, Sham, Titus, Calli, and Tayo. They're going to be here for a few rotations, and Ladinda and I thought that it would be nice if you all got to know each other. If you remember, Gren and Lawson were partnered when they were here."

"The only boy/girl partnering to make it all the way through the program," Angel said automatically. She had obviously heard a lot about them.

"We almost didn't make it," Lawson added. He glanced at Hutch, hoping that he wasn't about to say something wrong. "Hutch, even recommended that we be split up during our final orbit. That would have been terrible. Gren was my best friend when we were in school, and she's still my best friend now."

"We even apprentice together," Gren added.

"We're not you," Dod mumbled. It was the first time that he spoke.

"No," Lawson said quickly, "of course you're not. But when we were here, you and I were friends, weren't we? Wouldn't it be nice to hang out with someone who understands for a few rotations?"

"I guess." Dod didn't sound convinced.

"You'll get to miss your classes," Hutch added.

Dod seemed to brighten up. "Okay."

"Good." Hutch smiled. "Tell you what, why don't we all meet by the lake this afternoon? You can go for a hike and get to know each other. I'll have them pack a picnic for you. There's a beautiful spot on the far side of the lake that's easy to hike to. Sound good?"

"I'm willing to try," Angel said while Dod nodded.

"Angel and Dod, you're excused. I'll see you this afternoon." Hutch didn't say anything else until the two Purples were gone. "You six have your work cut out for you. As you can tell, they're not connecting. Gren and Lawson, you need to show them that a male/female partnering isn't the end of Terra. Calli and Tayo, let them see how close you are. Then fill them in on some of your past problems. Remember, though, that there are certain things that happened a couple of orbits ago that you still aren't to talk about."

"Um..." Sham started slowly, "what do you want Titus and me to do?"

"Just be yourselves. Show these two kids how to have fun. That's something that neither of them really know how to do right now." Hutch got up and slowly walked towards the door. "And Sham, try to not poke poor Calli too hard."

Chapter Nine

At the appointed time, Gren and her friends headed to the lake. Hutch was already there. "Here's your meal," he told them as he held up two backpacks. "It stays light fairly late so you should have plenty of time. Try to get the two kids to talk. There seems to be a lot of hostility, but I can't get either of them to tell me what is really going on."

"Have you wandered?" Lawson asked. He remembered one session from his final orbit where Hutch had found the information that he was looking for through a wandering session. It was not his favorite memory.

"That's a last resort," Hutch said. He looked off in the distance. "Here they come." Angel could clearly be seen. From far away she looked as if she could be related to Gren. Dod was with her, but he was several steps behind. He stared at the ground as he walked. Hutch raised his voice so that the two Purples could hear as they approached the group. "Right on time."

Angel stopped walking first. "We would have been here a few hundreds ago, but someone wasn't ready." There was hostility in her voice.

"I..." Dod protested but didn't say anything else.

"You're not late, we were early," Gren said as sweetly as possible. "Are you ready? It's a beautiful rotation for a hike."

"I'm ready," Angel replied. "I'm not so sure about Dod."

"Hey, I'm ready too!"

"I have some supplies for you," Hutch said. He handed one backpack to Lawson and the other to Sham.

"What about Titus?" Sham joked more to his friend than to

Hutch. "Why doesn't he have to carry anything?"

"You can trade off if it gets heavy," Hutch said. "I just figured that you wouldn't mind, since you love nature so much. You're probably used to hikes like this." He turned his attention to the entire group. "Take your time, and be back before dark. And be careful. It's mostly an easy hike but there are a couple of spots where the footing is rough. The path is clearly marked, but do any of you know the way?"

"I know it well," Gren said. It was a path that she had walked countless times in her orbits at the Learning Center. She would often go for a hike when she needed time alone.

"Meet me in my classroom when you're finished," Hutch instructed. "And have a good time!" He walked away, leaving the six Apprentices with the two Purples.

"Wait," Lawson said to Gren. "How do you know this path?"

"I used to walk it from time to time when we were students," she explained. "It's a good place to think."

"I didn't know that."

Gren smiled. "You don't know everything about me." She raised her voice. "Come on, everyone, let's get going."

Sham put on the pack. "Why does Hutch think that I love nature?" he asked out loud, but no one replied.

It did not take long for the eight hikers to break up into two groups. Gren and the other girls walked well in the lead, while the guys all lagged behind. Gren thought that it was a good time to try to get Angel to talk. She and the young girl were a few steps in front of Calli and Tayo. "You remind me so much of my little sister," Gren said. "You're an orbit older than she is. She's a Brown at the Culinary Institute this orbit."

"Do they have partnerships there?"

"Yeah. Winnie, that's my sister, is partnered with a girl named Mollie. They spent their school break with me when they were Whites." She didn't give any more information than that.

"It must be nice to be partnered with a girl."

"Just because they're both girls, doesn't make them great partners. They're great partners because they're friends."

"The fact that they're both girls, makes it easier."

"Not always. Calli and Tayo back there?" Gren pointed over her shoulder. "They used to fight like crazy. They were also not partnered when they were Whites, and when they did become partners it was because there were no other choices."

"They seem so close," Angel said.

"They are. But that's because they decided to work on the friendship. It wasn't until they learned to respect each other that they started to work together as a team. And look at me. Lawson and I were partnered as Whites, and his friendship is the best thing in my life." She glanced behind to make sure that Lawson wasn't close enough to hear, she didn't want it to go to his head.

"I remember when you and Lawson were here. You had a huge fight and they almost broke up your partnership."

"Friends fight sometimes. Lawson and I still fight on occasion. But I know that he has my back when I need him. I honestly can't imagine my life without him."

"I imagine my life without Dod all the time."

Lawson and Dod walked slightly ahead of Sham and Titus. Lawson decided to try to get Dod to open up to him. "So, Kid, what's going on? Why don't you like your partner?"

"I like her well enough," Dod explained. "She doesn't like me. She'd rather spend time with the girls and she doesn't care if we do anything together when we're not in class."

"So, everything is all her fault?"

"Yeah."

Lawson could tell that he had his work cut out for him.

· ə ɘ◯ə ə ·

Once they arrived at the correct spot, everyone sat down on the rocks. Angel sat on one end and Dod sat as far away from her as he could. Calli decided to sit next to Sham. She didn't feel like getting poked, but she thought that if the two Purples saw them getting along that they might put aside their thoughts about friends of the opposite gender for a few hundreds. She was grateful and slightly surprised when Sham didn't poke her. The group passed around the backpacks and everyone took some food. The silence was so thick that it could be felt.

"I love it up here," Gren said at last. "It's a great place to think." No one else said anything. "I used to come up here and dream about the future." She paused again and there were no replies. "What about you, Dod? What do you think that your future holds?"

"There are a couple of good Dream Wandering practices near where my parents live. I wouldn't mind apprenticing close to home."

"How about you, Angel?" Gren asked. "I know it's still several orbits away, but do you know where you want to apprentice?"

"My friends and I talk about that all the time. I have lots of friends who are girls."

Gren wondered if the silence had been better.

* ◦ ● ◖ ● ◦ ◦

Once the hike was over, the entire group returned to Hutch's classroom. He excused the two Purples. "So, what do you think?" he asked once the door was closed.

"There's a lot of hostility," Gren said. "I have a feeling that Angel's friends aren't helping. I know how she feels, I used to get teased about having a boy partner."

"You did?" Lawson seemed surprised.

"All the time, I just didn't tell you about it." Gren turned back towards Hutch. "I don't think that Dod did anything to get her angry. But she's insecure because a boy/girl partnering can be hard."

"Dod is just frustrated," Lawson added. "He blames everything on Angel."

Hutch thought for a micro. "Having them spend time with the six of you was a good idea. Tomorrow you'll have the entire rotation with them. Ladinda has come up with a surprise, and I think you'll all enjoy it. Get a good night's sleep, and we'll meet back here after the morning meal."

Chapter Ten

Everyone slept well that night, the fresh air and exercise had made them tired. In the morning, they met in the dining area. They all decided to have a good morning meal because they had no idea what Ladinda and Hutch had planned for them.

"I'm still not sure what we're doing here," Sham commented. He looked at Gren. "You and Lawson, yeah, but the rest of us? I didn't really feel all that useful on that hike."

"Maybe things will be different this rotation," Titus suggested.

"I don't know. And I'm still not sure why Hutch thinks that I love nature."

"Gren and I told him that when we saw him last orbit," Lawson said without further explanation.

"Look." Gren motioned with her head towards a group of Purple girls. Angel was right in the middle. "I guess everything I told her about how great it is to be partnered with a boy didn't sink in yet."

Lawson grinned. "What did you say?"

"I lied through my teeth."

"There's Dod," Calli pointed out. The young boy found a seat by himself and started to eat. He stared only at his food, he didn't look up.

"This is going to be a fun rotation," Sham said.

A unit later everyone met in Hutch's classroom. Both Ladinda and Hutch were already there. "I have a great surprise for all eight of you," Ladinda started. Her tone was even more cheerful than normal. "I've arranged for an all-rotation water craft ride! There is something special about the sea air, it can really help to clear your head."

"Sea air?" Gren repeated. "You mean we're not taking a water craft out on the lake?"

"No, Gren, this is going to be much more special than that. I had to pull some strings, but a friend is going to let you borrow his small water craft. You'll be out on the ocean for the entire rotation." Gren nodded, but didn't say anything else. She knew that Ladinda didn't have to pull those strings very hard. The woman was always able to get what she wanted. "Titus, your family owns a water craft, correct?"

"That's right, Ma'am. It's a MAAD-14."

"Are you licensed to operate it?"

"Yes, Ma'am."

"Good. This is an older model, it's a MAAD-06, but the basics will all be the same. Since you're licensed, my friend won't have to go along." Ladinda glanced around the room. "Is everyone ready? We have two glidemobiles with drivers set to take you to the ocean. It's a long ride, you'd better get going."

The girls rode in one glidemobile, the guys in the other. Gren sat next to Angel. Instead of bombarding the Purple with information on how great it could be to be partnered with a boy, she decided to make small talk. "So, have you ever been to the ocean before?"

"I've been there a few times with my family." Angel didn't seem to want to talk.

"What is your family like? Do you have any brothers or

sisters?"

"I have two sisters. I'm the youngest. One is two orbits older than I am and the other is four and a half."

"I have a little sister. She's quite a bit younger than I am, but we're still pretty close."

"Yeah, Winnie. You told me about her on the hike." Angel shifted her weight slightly and stared out the window. She hoped that her new body position would show Gren that she was not in the mood for conversation.

Gren quietly sighed and turned so that she could see out the window as well. Ladinda was right, it was going to be a long ride.

In the other glidemobile it was Titus and Sham who were doing most of the talking. "Are you going to let me help you with the controls?" Sham asked.

"We'll see," Titus replied. "I've never even seen one of the older models, I'm not sure how different it's going to be from my parents' water craft."

"Your dad would let me steer."

Titus laughed. "My dad would never let you steer!"

Dod looked at Lawson. "Are they always like this?"

Lawson nodded. "You'll get used to them after a while."

It took over three units to get to the marina but it felt much longer. They got out of the glidemobiles and the two drivers took off immediately, leaving the group of eight not knowing where they were supposed to go. A hundred later they were approached by an older man. He was too well dressed to be at a marina. "You the group from the Learning Center?"

Gren decided to take charge. "Yes, we are. I'm Gren, and these are..."

The man cut her off. "I'm Ward. Ladinda told me that you were coming. Who is it who also owns a MAAD?"

Titus raised his hand. "That would be me. Well, my parents own it, but I've spent a lot of time in it."

"What model?"

"14."

"This is an 06. Come with me, Kid, we need to go over the controls. The rest of you can wait here."

"What about me?" Sham asked. "I'm going to help him steer!"

"The rest of you can wait here," Ward repeated sternly. He walked away and Titus needed to run to catch up with him.

● ○ ○●○ ○ ●

Half a unit later Titus and Ward returned. The rest of the group was ready to leave. "I'm all set," Titus said. "We've got some supplies on board, for when we get hungry."

"I'm hungry now," Sham mumbled, but everyone ignored him.

Chapter Eleven

The water craft was a bit rundown. Ward gave everyone a quick tour, it didn't take long. He gave Titus some final instructions. Sham listened as closely as Titus did. Ward then asked to see if anyone had any questions. When there were none, he left. "Take good care of my baby," he called from the dock, taking one last look back.

A few hundreds later they were on their way. Titus was on the bridge at the controls, Sham and Dod were at his side. The girls and Lawson all sat on the deck. It already felt like a long rotation, and their journey had barely started. Since Lawson had had very little interaction with Angel so far, he decided to see if he could get to know her better. "So, Angel," he started, raising his voice so that he could be heard over the engine, "is this your first time on a water craft?"

Angel looked around. "It isn't much of a water craft."

She was right. The vessel was a lot smaller than Lawson had expected it to be. He had seen pictures of the model that Titus' family owned and that wasn't much like the water craft that they were on. There was a cramped area underneath that contained sleeping quarters, the engine room, and a necessary room. There was also a very small cooking area. The deck that Lawson sat on with the girls was rather plain. The open bridge was on a third level. That was small as well. "That's true," Lawson said at last. "But it's better than classes, right?"

"I'd rather be in class," Angel snapped back. "I'm missing a lot because of this, and I'm going to get behind. This is so stupid."

Lawson realized that Angel had changed quite a bit since he

knew her as a White. He didn't know what had caused the division between her and Dod, but he was sure that it was mostly Angel's fault. "There's more to life than classes."

Gren decided to step in. "If Ladinda thought that it was going to hurt your studies to have you miss a few rotations, she never would allow it. She really does have your best interests in mind." She and Lawson exchanged a knowing glance.

"Whatever."

Lawson decided to change the subject. "Did you see the cooking area?" he asked Gren. "I'd love to see what Winnie could do with that!" He turned his attention back to Angel. "Winnie is..."

"Gren's little sister. I know."

Suddenly spending time at work, getting ready for the Trials and listening to Haas be critical, didn't sound too bad to Lawson.

On the bridge, Sham was trying to make himself useful. He looked at the map. "Are you sure you know how to read this thing?"

"Sham," Titus said, "I know what I'm doing." He turned his attention to Dod. "Have you ever been on a water craft before?"

Dod shook his head no. "I've never even seen the ocean."

"Tell you what. You can be my navigator. Sham, give Dod the map."

"Yes, Sir, Captain." Sham saluted, then handed over the map.

"Captain Titus!" Dod repeated. He started to laugh. It was the first time that they had seen the child laugh.

A unit into their ride Sham decided to join the rest of the

group. "Captain Titus won't let me do anything." He took a seat next to Calli. "He's named Dod our Navigator."

"Then we're all in trouble," Angel mumbled.

"He's doing a great job," Sham said. "We're set on autopilot anyway, there's not really anything to do." He looked away from Calli but jabbed his finger into her arm. "Poke."

"You're not allowed to touch anyone of the opposite gender," Angel quickly said.

"No," Sham corrected, "you're not allowed to touch a student of the opposite gender when you're also a student. I graduated two orbits ago, Calli last orbit. So, I can now do this..." He poked Calli several times.

Calli smiled. "And I can do this." She grabbed Sham's finger and bent it back slightly. She made sure that she didn't hurt him, but she also made her point. She then let go and moved to the seat next to Angel. "See what you have to look forward to?"

"I don't understand that rule," Angel said.

"You're not supposed to," Gren added quickly. "Lawson and I struggled with it the entire time we were at the Learning Center. It didn't seem fair that other students could hug their partners when happy or put an arm around each other when sad, but I could be expelled if I gave my partner as much as a pat on the back after a good wandering session."

"I always hated that rule," Lawson added.

Gren laughed. "But we made it without breaking it. I think that in some ways it brought us closer. I don't know why Ladinda comes up with some of her ideas, but I do know that she does what she does because she cares so much."

"Oh, is that what it is," Lawson teased. "I thought that she just liked tormenting me." He and Gren shared a smile.

"See, that's what I don't understand," Angel said. "You two are obviously close. How did that happen? How can you even stand to be in the same room with each other?"

For the first time, Gren felt like they were making progress. "Lawson and I are friends. We found common ground early on. We both wanted to make it work in the program, so we decided to get along. We got teased, a lot at first, but we did our best to ignore it. When I was your age I thought that it would be nice to be partnered with a girl instead..."

"Hey!"

"...but eventually I realized that working with Lawson gave me an advantage. I could see things through a male point of view, which was something that none of the other girls could do. I think that I'm a better Wanderer because of it."

"What did you do when the other girls would tease you?" Angel asked.

"Sometimes I'd joke about it. I'd tell them that they were just jealous because Lawson was kind of cute when he was younger. Other times I would just tell them to stop. There wasn't anything that I could do about my partnership, so I told the other girls that they should not even mention it. I lost a couple of friends because of it, but then I realized that they weren't really my friends."

"Oh."

"It's not easy, Angel." Gren smiled again. "But it is worth it."

The water craft shook violently, and then it was quiet. A few micros later Titus and Dod ran down the stairs from the bridge. Dod still held the map. "Guys..." Titus started slowly, "...we have a problem."

Chapter Twelve

The water craft's engine had been loud since the micro they boarded, but it was suddenly silent. Everyone in the group stared at Titus. "We've lost power," he explained.

"Dod, what did you do?" Angel asked.

"I didn't do anything!"

"He didn't do anything," Titus echoed. "Sham, I need you to take a look at the fuel cell with me. Maybe it's a simple connection problem." Sham got up and followed Titus. Dod took a seat. He continued to study the map.

Lawson was painfully aware that he was the only adult male who was not trying to help fix the vessel. He also knew that he would be in the way if he joined Sham and Titus. "They'll find the problem," he said, trying to lighten the mood. He wished that he felt as confident as he sounded.

It took less than a hundred for Titus to find the source of the problem. "The fuel cell is shot," he said. "See for yourself."

Sham took a look. "Shouldn't you have checked that before we left?"

"I thought Ward had looked everything over! I assumed that he wouldn't let us leave otherwise!"

"Yeah, you'd think," Sham said. "Wait, we'll just send a transmission. Let the Sea Protectors know that we're in trouble. They'll send a ship to rescue us, and we'll be back at the Learning Center before the evening meal. Easy solution."

"Easy, except I already tried that. There's a short in the

transmitter line. That's not working either, incoming and outgoing transmissions are both fried."

"So, what do we do?" Sham was worried, but tried not to let it show.

"We tell everyone else what is going on. We've been in jams before, with the whole group back together we should be able to figure something out."

* * * ● ● ● * *

On the deck, the silence was deafening. Angel was so nervous that she was shaking. Gren moved and sat next to her. She put her arm around the young Purple. "We'll be fine," she said.

Even though they were gone for only a few hundreds, it seemed like forever until Sham and Titus returned. "It's the fuel cell," Titus explained. "It looks like there was a power surge. That's why we shook like we did. We have some backup power, but it's not enough to get us back to shore. The transmitter also isn't working, so we can't let anyone know our position. Right now, we're just drifting."

"Here," Dod said. He still had his face buried in the map. "There's an island. I think it's uninhabited. Would we have enough backup power to make it?"

Titus walked over to Dod and looked at the spot on the map. "I think we would. That's a very good idea, Dod."

"Wouldn't it make more sense to stay where we are?" Angel asked.

"No," Titus quickly replied. "If we're drifting or just sitting in the ocean, no one will ever know where to look for us. We need to stay in one place where it's logical for the Sea Protectors to search, and this is the best way to do it. Dod, you might have just saved us."

"How far away is it?" Tayo asked.

Titus looked at the map again. "Probably a unit or so. We have to get to work. Dod, come help me at the controls. We need to make sure that we're heading in the right direction."

A unit later something green could be seen off in the distance. Everyone put on their safety vests, just in case. Titus was able to get the water craft close to shore, but there wasn't a suitable place to dock it. He let down the anchor and then returned to his friends. "I think I know why no one lives here," Titus said. "There's no decent place to dock. We're going to have to swim to shore. Sham, Lawson, help me get the supplies. There are some waterproof containers that we can use. We'll get everything off that we can."

"Wouldn't it make more sense to just stay here?" Calli asked.

Titus shook his head. "Did you hear that grinding noise a few hundreds ago? There was a rocky patch that we scraped through. I don't know if the integrity of the hull was damaged, but I don't think we should take any chances. We'll be safer on shore."

Gren turned towards Angel. "Do you know how to swim?" Angel nodded. "Good. My little sister Winnie didn't learn until recently."

Even though Angel was nervous, the comment irritated her. "Gren, I am not your little sister."

Gren wasn't sure how to reply, so she didn't say anything. She hadn't meant to treat Angel as if she were Winnie, but realized that she had compared the two several times already.

"Lawson, Sham," Titus said again, "come on. We need to see how much stuff we can salvage. Gren, wait for us. We should all make it to shore together."

There wasn't much on the water craft in the way of supplies. The waterproof containers were designed to float. They filled the containers with food, there was enough to last for several rotations. They also found an emergency kit and some blankets, some cooking and dining items, and a few other things that they thought might be useful. After they had looked through everything, Titus, Sham, and Lawson rejoined the rest of the group. "Everyone ready?" Titus asked. He took a portable rope ladder and dropped it over the side. "I'll go first. Gren, you follow me when I call. Then Calli, Tayo, Angel, and Dod. I'll get them to shore. Sham and Lawson, you hold back. I'll then come back and we'll get the supplies. Sound good?"

"Good, no," Sham replied. "But I can't think of anything else that we can do."

Titus climbed down the ladder and lowered himself into the water. "Come on Gren," he called. "At least the water is a comfortable temperature!"

Gren climbed down the ladder, and then the rest of the first group followed. It wasn't a far swim, but it was tiring. Titus returned and then helped Sham and Lawson with the supplies. Soon everyone was safely on shore.

"Now what do we do?" Angel asked. She was shivering.

"There's a fire starter in the emergency kit," Titus said. There was plenty of driftwood on the beach near where they were sitting. "We'll start a fire and all dry off and warm up." He got up to gather a few pieces of fuel. Sham sprang to his feet and helped him.

"How are we going to let anyone know where we are?" was Angel's next question.

"We'll wander," Gren said quietly. She turned towards her friends. "Do you remember what Ladinda told us when we arrived? She gave us permission to wander. She didn't mention Angel and Dod exclusively, so technically we have permission to wander anyone at the Learning Center."

"It's so far away," Angel said.

"And Angel and I have barely begun to learn about wandering," Dod added.

"Wandering distances is easy with practice," Gren said with a smile. "And believe me, I've had a lot of practice. Sleep tonic leaves traces. That will make it easier to find the Learning Center because they use so much. We'll just keep popping into dreams until someone realizes what's going on. If we can find a dream that Hutch is wandering, he'll know what to do." Gren sat back and sighed in relief. She knew that it wasn't a foolproof plan, but at least it was something.

Chapter Thirteen

It didn't take long for the group to decide upon some simple rules. The most important one was that no one was to go off alone. They would stay on the beach, but if anyone did leave for some reason it would always be with a partner. There weren't a lot of supplies, but they also knew that they had everything that they would need for a few rotations. There was a fair amount of food, some cooking equipment, ten blankets, and the emergency kit. The fire helped everyone to dry off.

Lawson looked through the kit. "We have two analyzers. That's good news."

"What's an analyzer?" Dod asked.

"It analyzes food and water," Lawson explained. "It will tell us what is safe to eat and drink." He continued to rummage. "There are also some safety tabs." He looked at Dod again. "Those are to clean the water if it's not safe. You add a tab, boil the water for a few hundreds, then check again with the analyzer. In most cases a tab will make the water drinkable."

"When did you learn all this?" Gren asked.

Lawson smiled at his former partner. "After what we've been through the past couple of orbits, I decided that it was a good idea to be ready for anything, so I've been brushing up on my survival skills."

"What have you been through?" Dod asked.

"We haven't eaten anything since this morning," Calli said, quickly changing the subject. There was one life changing event that they weren't allowed to talk about, and another that they didn't like to mention too often. "Maybe we should have something. We need to keep up our strength."

Everyone else agreed that it was a good idea. Since they had some cooking utensils and plates, they made a hot meal. As they sat near the fire they passed around the food. No one took too much because they weren't sure how long they would be there and they didn't want to run out.

"We need to make a plan, and keep it simple," Titus said. "I think we should all get a good night's sleep tonight. Once the sun goes down we're not going to be able to do any exploring, and we don't want to risk anyone getting lost in the dark, so we'll leave that until morning. No one ever goes off alone. If for some reason someone does get lost, we'll communicate by wandering."

"How can you wander without sleep tonic?" Angel asked.

"It's not difficult," Gren said. "Lawson and I do it all the time. He'll let his mind drift and end up in a dream-like state. I'll then wander, and we communicate that way."

"Sounds hard," Angel commented.

"It helps to really know and trust each other," Lawson said. "Gren knows what to look for because she knows me better than anyone."

"What about Hutch?" Angel asked. "Are you going to try to communicate with him soon?"

"There wouldn't be any wandering sessions going on right now," Gren said. "I'll have to wait until there are classes going on tomorrow."

After everyone had finished eating they agreed that it was time to get some sleep. They designated two different necessary areas; one for the boys and the other for the girls. Everyone took a blanket.

"There are two blankets left over," Sham commented.

"Angel should have one," Dod said quickly. "She was shivering earlier."

"Fine with me." Sham handed one blanket to Angel. "Anyone else?" No one said anything. Sham handed the other blanket to Calli. "Why don't you take it?"

Calli glanced around. No one else seemed to want the extra blanket, so she accepted it. "Thanks."

Sham started to walk away. He waited until Calli's attention was elsewhere, then he snuck up behind her. "Poke."

Calli glared at Sham. "Just wait until tomorrow."

The sun set and the fire burned out as well. They tried to settle down for the night. The beauty of the location was not lost on any of them. The air temperature was comfortable, and the stars were incredible. If they had to be marooned, they had found an ideal place to be stuck for a while.

· ○ ○◉○ ○ ·

Angel's head was beneath the water. She tried desperately to swim to the surface, but something kept pulling her down. "Let go of the extra baggage," a soothing voice said. "It's weighing you down."

Angel tried to say something but ended up with a mouthful of water.

"Don't talk, just let go of the baggage. Then you'll be able to swim to the surface."

Angel looked down and realized that her arms were full of travel cases. She let go of them and was able to get her head above the water.

"Swim to shore." Angel did as instructed. As she climbed out of the water she started to cough. "There's no reason to cough, you can breathe normally."

"Gren?" Angel had recognized the voice but wanted confirmation.

"I'm here for you," Gren's voice said. "You know who else is here for you?"

"Who?"

"Dod. Trust him. Your friends back at the Learning Center aren't going to be able to help you through this, but Dod will. You need to start working together as a team."

"But..."

"No," Gren's voice said sternly. "This is not open for debate. You and Dod are partners, and you need to work together."

"I'll try."

"Good. Now get some sleep, and dream only about nice things. No more nightmares."

. . . . . ● ○ ● ○ ● ○ . . . .

Gren smiled as she exited the dream. She didn't know if anything that she said would make a difference, but she hoped that maybe she had helped the young Purple. She wondered if Lawson had wandered Dod's dream as well.

Chapter Fourteen

It was a long night, but somehow everyone was able to get some sleep. In the morning the group sat in a circle and shared the morning meal. They talked about what their next steps should be. They decided to break into two groups, since they had two analyzers. That way they would be able to look for food and water, just in case they needed more. They agreed to try to wander from time to time so that they could keep in touch. They would also attempt to touch dreams at the Learning Center. They knew that Gren had the best chance of actually communicating with someone back there, but that all six Apprentices still needed to try.

"So," Calli said, "how are we going to do this? Groups by gender?"

"I think we should do it by partners, or former partners," Gren added quickly. "I'd like Angel and Dod to be with Lawson and me. I thought maybe we could show them a little bit about communicating through wandering."

Calli sighed. "Okay."

Sham grinned and put his arm around Calli's shoulders. "Looks like you're stuck with Titus and me."

"Great," Calli said as she pulled away. "Let's get going. So, we'll meet back here in about three units?"

"Yeah," Lawson replied. "Hopefully we'll have some good news by then."

As the groups started walking off in two different directions, Calli loudly said to her best friend, "So, Tayo, when is Grey coming to visit again? You're so lucky that his former partner lives close to us so he can visit whenever he wants."

"I don't want to have to hear about Grey this whole time," Sham protested. "It's bad enough that I have to see him at work. Why Cassidy decided to keep him as an Associate..."

○ ○ ●◉● ○ ○

Gren, Lawson, Angel, and Dod headed off in a different direction. There wasn't a path, but the area wasn't too overgrown so the walk was not difficult. Gren and Angel walked well in front of Lawson and Dod. "Kind of makes you long for the path that we were on a couple of rotations ago, doesn't it?"

"I still don't understand why all this is going on," Angel said. "Why can't Dod and I just be in school like everyone else? And why did Ladinda bring you here?"

"Because working well with your partner is the most important part of your education," Gren said. "You're not yet to the point where you're wandering each other's dreams. By the time you get to the practical classes, you need to trust your partner with your deepest secrets. Quite honestly, Angel, you don't even act like you like Dod, let alone are willing to trust him. Do you want to become a licensed Dream Wanderer?"

"Of course, I do!" Angel seemed a little bit upset by the quiz.

"Then you need to learn to work with your partner. If Ladinda didn't think that you and Dod were a good fit, she'd have changed your partnership a long time ago. But if you don't at least make an effort to get along..." Gren let her sentence drop.

"What?"

"It's no coincidence that each class is smaller than the one an orbit behind it."

"Do you really think that they would kick us out of the program?"

Gren stopped and lowered her voice. "Not both of you. From what I've seen, it looks like Dod is at least making an effort."

"I...I..." Angel stomped off in front of Gren.

● ○ ●◉● ○ ●

"Lawson, can I ask you a question?"

"Ask me anything, Kid." From where they were they could see Gren and Angel, but couldn't hear what they were saying. It looked like Angel was upset about something.

"Did you have it this hard? Did Gren hate you for no reason?"

Lawson grinned. "That's two questions, Kid. But things were a little bit different with Gren and me. She was always so focused on her studies that she would have done anything that they told her to do. If they had told Gren that she needed to partner with a jick, she would have done it."

Dod shuddered at the thought of the small insect. "I hate jicks."

"Me too. And so does Gren. But my point is that Gren is a 'follow the rules' type of person. She did what she was told that she was supposed to do, and she still does. But that's not saying that it was always easy. Gren and I faced our own set of problems."

"Like what?"

Lawson smiled. "You'll know when you're older." He stared at Gren in the distance. "One thing that made it a little bit easier to bond was the fact that I always spent my breaks with her family. They took me in and made me feel at home."

"Why didn't you spend them with your own family?" Dod asked.

"Don't have one. I was orphaned pretty young and became a

ward of the Learning Center. Ladinda was my legal guardian until I became an adult." Lawson laughed. "Can you imagine spending breaks with her? I was pretty lucky that Gren's family is so great. They always treated me like I belonged. They still do."

"Lawson, Dod," Gren called loudly, "come see what we found!"

Lawson and Dod ran to see what was so interesting. As they passed a group of trees they saw a clearing. There was a small waterfall and a stream, with a watering hole on the side. "Wow," Lawson said, "I wonder if the water is clean. If it is, we can fill up the bottles and take them back to our camp." He pulled out the analyzer and tested the water in the pool. "Looks good." He lost his footing and tumbled into the water.

Gren laughed. She held out her hand. "Here, I'll pull you out." Lawson took her hand. He tugged hard and Gren flew into the water as well. "Hey!"

"Play along," Lawson whispered. "These two need to learn how to have fun."

"I'll get you out," Dod said. He didn't even make it far enough to reach out his hand. He slipped on a wet rock and tumbled into the water as well.

Angel stood on the side. The group in the water started to splash each other. They were all laughing. "Oh, why not," she said at last. She joined them in the water. It wasn't deep, it went up to her shoulders. She immediately splashed Dod, who did the same back to her.

Gren grinned at Lawson. It was the first time that they had seen the two Purples get along. "I need to see if I can find someone at the Learning Center," she said.

"I'll help." Lawson got out of the water with her, knowing that there was nothing that he could do to help. Angel and Dod stayed in the water and continued to play. Gren and Lawson found a place to sit in the sun so that they could dry off. "That's good to see, they're finally acting like kids."

Gren nodded. "I agree, but next time find a way for them to get along that doesn't include my getting soaked, okay?"

Lawson grinned. He had enjoyed pulling Gren into the water a little bit too much. "I'll try. What did you say to Angel before? We could see that she was upset about something."

"I told her that if she doesn't start trying to get along with Dod that she'll get kicked out of the program. What were you and Dod talking about?"

"I said that you would have agreed to be partnered with a jick if that was what Ladinda had wanted."

Gren patted Lawson on the leg. "You were a much better partner than a jick."

"I bet you didn't always feel that way."

"No comment." Gren and Lawson both laughed. Suddenly aware of how close they were sitting, Lawson moved slightly closer. A micro before they could kiss, Gren moved away. "Lawson, we can't. You know that as well as I do. If Haas were to find out, we'd both be dismissed. We can't let that happen, not when we're so close to getting what we've always wanted."

Lawson purposely put distance between himself and Gren. "What we've always wanted? Isn't it all about what you've always wanted?"

"What are you talking about?"

Lawson sighed. "So, after we've passed the Trials and are licensed, what will your excuse be then?"

"I'm not making excuses, I'm following the rules!"

"Yeah, Gren, you and your rules." Lawson took a deep breath and let it out slowly. "You should try to make contact. I'll see if I can find Sham or someone, tell them that we found water."

"Lawson..."

Lawson had his eyes closed. Gren knew that he was trying to get into a dream-like state. It was the best way to communicate with the others on the island. Gren took a quick peek inside of his dream. "I'm sorry," she whispered. She then reached out to see if she could find a wandering session at the Learning Center. She wasn't exactly sure where to look, but she knew to look for sleep tonic. Sleep tonic left traces behind that a Wanderer could pick up on, so if there was a lot of tonic used in one place, there was a good chance that it was the Learning Center.

Chapter Fifteen

At the appointed time everyone gathered on the beach once again. Tayo had been able to wander Lawson's dream so her group knew that the others had found water. She, in turn, let Lawson know that her group had found some edible food. They weren't to the point where they were running out, but it was nice to know that there was something else to eat if needed.

Gren kept looking at Lawson, but he kept his distance. He wasn't in the mood to deal with what had almost happened. He was upset but not surprised. Gren treasured following the rules more than just about anything. Lawson sometimes wondered if the rules were more important to her than he was.

Since she wasn't doing anything else, Calli decided to prepare a meal. She was hungry, so she knew that everyone else probably was as well. She was the only one who had eaten any of the food that they had found. No one in her group wanted to try something unknown, so they played a game. Calli was the loser, so she ate one of the root vegetables. It tasted terrible. She was glad that they had plenty of other food.

Sham had built a fire and Angel and Dod sat near it to dry off. It was the closest that they had sat next to each other since everyone arrived at the Learning Center. Lawson sat down near them.

After looking at Lawson several more times Gren decided to sit near the fire as well. She was mostly dry but the warmth felt good. She closed her eyes and tried to wander again.

"How does she do it?" Angel asked. "I mean, we're so far from the Learning Center. How does she even know what to look for?"

"Gren is great at wandering distances," Lawson explained. "It's something that she perfected in our final orbit."

"How did she learn it?" was Angel's next question.

"Necessity," Lawson explained without giving any further details.

"I have a question," Dod said. "That thing that you were doing before, when you contacted Tayo. Can you teach us to do it?"

"It's pretty easy," Lawson said, "but you really need to trust each other in order for it to work. Do you think that you and Angel can trust each other that much?" Both Purples nodded. "Okay. Dod, close your eyes." The young boy did as instructed. "Now relax, and think about something fun. Something that you really enjoy doing. Imagine yourself doing it. Let your mind drift and live in that micro." Lawson turned his attention to Angel. "Now it's your turn. Wander his dream."

"We don't know how to wander yet. We just know how to touch dreams, not how to enter them."

"So, touch his dream. At least it will be a beginning. Then, when you're older and you're wandering, you'll be able to communicate like this. That is, if you're still partners. If you've been split up you won't be allowed to wander each other."

"I..."

"Just try to touch the dream, Angel. I guarantee you that what I am teaching you right now is a lot more important than the classes that you're missing back at the Learning Center."

"Okay," Angel said at last. "I'll try." Angel closed her eyes. Fifteen micros later she opened them again. "I did it! I saw a glimpse of Dod's dream!"

"Great job, Angel!" Lawson turned his attention to Dod. "You can stop dreaming now."

Dod opened his eyes. "I think I felt you there."

"That boy that you were playing with," Angel said. "Who is he?"

"That's my brother," Dod replied.

Angel looked confused. "I didn't know that you have a brother."

"You never asked me about my family."

· ◦ ● ⬤ ● ◦ ·

Gren sat with her eyes closed. She had found a small trace of tonic, but she had no way of knowing whether or not it was from the Learning Center. She had hoped that she would be able to find traces from a large amount of tonic because the Learning Center used so much. She couldn't wander just any dream, that was against the rules. She couldn't break the rules, especially when they were so close to getting everything that they had always wanted.

With her eyes still closed Gren replayed her previous conversation with Lawson in her mind. Did he not have the same goals that she had? She knew that he had accepted the apprenticeship with Haas so that they could still be together. He would have much preferred to gain practical experience with someone like Cassidy. Still, working with Haas had been wonderful for both of them. The simple fact that they were the first Apprentices that Haas had taken on in decades was going to hold a lot of weight when it came time to look for a permanent job.

What kind of practice would Lawson want to work for after being licensed? Gren had always assumed that they would work together. Deep down she hoped that Haas was going to offer her an Associate position, she loved the thought of the prestige that a job in his practice would bring. Would he offer one to Lawson as well? If so, that meant that the two of them could never let their relationship develop, because Haas strictly forbid inter-office dating. Would Lawson give up his career for her? She had no doubt that he would. Would she do the same for him? She didn't know the answer to that question.

When they were students, Lawson would joke that he planned to become a "wandering Dream Wanderer". Lawson said that he wanted to travel Terra and see all that the planet had to offer. He had put that dream on hold for her. Gren knew how Lawson felt about her. The problem was that she didn't know how much she was willing to sacrifice for him.

"Any luck?" Titus' voice scared Gren.

"Just one trace of tonic. I don't think it was from the Learning Center."

"I'm sure that they're looking for us by now." Titus handed Gren a plate of food. "Here, you need to keep your strength up."

"Thanks." Gren took the food but she didn't feel much like eating.

Chapter Sixteen

After the meal, Dod walked down close to the ocean. He stayed where he could see the others. He sat on the edge of where the wet and dry sand met. He started to make a shape in the wet sand. Angel walked down and sat next to him. "Want some help?" she asked. "Maybe we could build a sand sculpture or something."

"Sure," Dod said. He had a couple of sticks and he handed one to his partner. "These are kind of fun to dig with."

"Thanks." Angel took the stick and started to scribble in the wet sand. "I can't believe that we've been partnered all this time and I never asked you if you have a brother. I guess I haven't been making as much of an effort as I thought."

Dod smiled. "I have a sister too. She's just a baby. She was born right before we started this orbit so I haven't spent all that much time with her."

Angel seemed surprised. "You have a baby sister? I love babies."

"Maybe when we get back to the Learning Center you can meet her," Dod suggested. "My family doesn't live too far away. It's not hard to visit them for a couple of units."

"I'd like that."

Sham watched the two young Purples from a distance. Part of him was keeping an eye on them because they were close to the water, but mostly he was glad to see them getting along. Gren still sat near the dying fire, trying to wander. Lawson was far away from Gren. He sat in the sand, he looked like he was searching as well. Sham couldn't see Tayo but assumed that she was also looking for the Learning Center. Calli was picking up pieces of wood for their next fire. Sham glanced around, trying to find his own former partner. "Titus, where are you?" He waited for a few micros, then called again. "Titus?"

"I'm over here." Titus was sitting on the ground, barely within sight.

Sham walked over to him. "What are you doing over here?"

"I'm trying to make contact with the Learning Center."

"Gren's trying to find them," Sham said. "Lawson and Tayo are as well, but if anyone is going to be able to find Hutch, it's Gren."

"Yeah, well maybe I thought that it was about time that someone besides Gren gets the glory." There was a harshness in Titus' tone that Sham wasn't used to.

"What's your problem?"

Titus sighed. "I'm the one who got us into this mess. I guess I want to do whatever I can to get us out. So, let me try, okay? Why don't you go bother Calli or something?"

"That's a good idea. I'll let you get back to what you were doing." Sham walked away. "Hey Calli!"

Calli put the wood in her arms in a pile on the ground as Sham approached. "Look, Sham, I'm really not in the mood for a poke war right now."

Sham held up his hands. "Okay, truce...for now. Besides, there's something going on that's even more important than irritating you."

"Wow, it must be pretty big."

Sham grinned. "Come with me." They took a few steps before

Sham pointed at the two Purples. They were working together to build something in the sand. "Look at them. They're actually having fun."

"At least something good is coming out of this trip."

"They'll find us Calli," Sham said. "We've been in worse situations than this."

"That's not what I'm worried about. Have you noticed how Gren and Lawson are acting? I think that something is wrong."

"It's a little more intense than usual, but this is perfectly normal for them. Remember, Titus and I live with Lawson. We're used to having to deal with Gren's moods."

Calli took a step away. "It's all Gren's fault?"

Sham shook his head. "Not at all. But this is the closest that they've ever been to having to deal with 'it'." He made quotation marks with his fingers as he said the word. "Lawson sees things a lot more clearly than Gren does. In his mind they'll pass the Trials and then 'it' will finally become a reality. Gren is focused on the Trials, and I think that 'it' is something that she wants to put off as long as possible. Titus and I agree that after they're licensed, Gren is going to say that she needs to focus on getting her career started. She'll want to put 'it' off for a while longer."

"You and Titus talk about Gren and Lawson?"

"If you lived with Lawson, you'd understand. He's doing really well with Haas, and that surprises me sometimes because he thinks about 'it' more than he does his job."

"So, what exactly do you mean by 'it'?" Calli asked. She made the same gesture with her fingers.

Sham grinned and put his arm around Calli's shoulders. "Calli, Calli, Calli. You know exactly what 'it' I'm talking about." He leaned even closer and whispered in her ear. "It's the same 'it' that you and I are going to have to deal with one of these rotations." He removed his arm and took a step away. "I'm gonna go bug Titus. I'll talk to you later."

As Sham walked away, Calli stared after him. She had no idea what had just happened.

Chapter Seventeen

Although she spent all afternoon trying to wander, Gren didn't have any luck. In the evening they built another fire and sat down to eat. Lawson was still upset with Gren, but he tried not to let it show. He didn't want to ruin the obvious progress that Angel and Dod were making. Lawson found it ironic that the Purples, who were there because they weren't connecting, were getting along better than he was with his best friend and former partner.

"I don't get it," Gren said. "I've been looking for large amounts of tonic. I've seen a little bit in different places, but not enough to ever make me think that it's at the Learning Center. I can't just pop into any dream, but I know that if I can find Hutch that he'll figure out what to do."

"I didn't even find any tonic," Tayo added, "but I'm not as good at distances as you are. Did you find anything, Lawson?"

Lawson shook his head but didn't say a word.

"How about you, Titus?" Sham asked. He sat across from Calli. "Did you have any luck?"

"I didn't know you were trying to find the Learning Center, Titus," Gren said.

"I thought I'd give it a try," Titus explained. He kept his head down. "I didn't find anything, though."

"So, what are we going to do?" Angel asked. "If we can't contact them, how will they ever find us?"

"We'll keep trying," Gren assured her. "The timing has been off, but we'll make contact eventually."

"Plus, if they think logically, they'll know to look for us here,"

Dod added. "It makes sense, given the course that we planned to take. You don't have to worry, Angel. We'll be fine."

"Thanks." Angel smiled at her partner. "I can't wait until we get home. I have a baby to meet."

"Huh?" Sham looked confused.

"Dod's little sister," Angel explained. "He doesn't live too far from the Learning Center, and his parents have told him that I'm welcome to come by for the evening meal anytime. I can't wait to meet the baby. And Dod's family. He's been telling me a lot about them this rotation."

Calli tried hard not to look at Sham. His earlier comment had surprised her, and she didn't know how she felt. She wasn't even sure that he had been serious, he might have been joking. She couldn't help but wonder if they even had an "it" to figure out. She had always thought that Sham was attractive, but then again so were both Lawson and Titus. She didn't have an "it" with either of them. Sham was never serious about anything. She didn't know why this was any different. True, they flirted from time to time, but she had never thought of it as anything more than just a game that they played.

"You're awfully quiet, Calli," Tayo said. "Everything okay?"

Calli nodded, but didn't say anything.

"She's thinking about a conversation that we had earlier," Sham said nonchalantly. "It was pretty deep, and extremely important. Wasn't it, Calli?"

Calli looked up for the first time in a while. "I'm sorry, Sham, did you say something?" Sham smiled and winked at her, and she instantly knew that he had been serious. Her heart melted. Maybe they did have an "it" after all.

"Excuse me," Lawson said as he stood up, "I'm going for a

walk by the water."

Gren jumped to her feet. "I'll go with you."

"No, that's okay, you can stay here."

"I thought we had a rule that no one would go away alone," Dod said, unaware of the tension between Gren and Lawson.

Gren looked at him. "He's right, Lawson."

"Fine. Let's go."

• ◦ ◖●◗ ◦ •

The water wasn't far away, and the two Apprentices walked silently. They stood at the water's edge for several hundreds and still didn't talk. Gren finally decided to say something. "At least we found a beautiful place to get stuck this time. It's not always raining, like it was on our adventure during our final orbit at the Learning Center."

"Yeah." Lawson started to walk.

"Lawson, are you ever going to forgive me? I didn't mean to hurt you."

"There's nothing to forgive, Gren," Lawson said. "You were just following the rules. You wouldn't be you if you didn't. It's just... I don't know. I guess I'm tired of letting the rules rule our lives. If we're just going to be friends I'll find a way to somehow live with that. But you need to let me know so that I can move on."

"Move on?"

"Not with someone else, I didn't mean it like that. I meant emotionally. I want you in my life, Gren. You're my best friend, you always have been. Your family has accepted me as family as well. I need you in my life, and I'll take you whatever way I can get you. I'm not asking you to make a decision right now. I know that you're feeling the pressure of the Trials, and I can also see how frustrated you are because you haven't contacted Hutch. Just don't lead me on for too long. I don't think I can continue on in limbo forever."

"Lawson, I..."

Lawson cut her off. "No decisions right now. But when you think about your future, try to include a thought or two about what my place in it might be. That's all I ask right now."

"But Lawson..."

"It's getting late. We should probably rejoin the group."

Lawson walked a step or two ahead of Gren. She had something that she wanted to say, but he hadn't given her a chance. The most confusing thing in her life had suddenly become crystal clear.

Chapter Eighteen

It took Gren forever to fall asleep. There was so much that she wanted to say to Lawson, but the timing hadn't been right and they needed to speak alone. She was a logical thinker and she knew that she needed to concentrate on contacting the Learning Center and getting everyone home again, that had to be her first priority. The girls had made their camp in one area, the guys slept not too far away. Gren gazed in the distance and in the starlight she could see that Lawson was sound asleep. She wondered if he was dreaming, but decided against finding out. Communicating with each other through dreams while letting their minds wander was one thing. If she were to just show up in his dream for no real reason, she would be invading his privacy. Dreams contained people's most inward thoughts, and she knew that Lawson's dream was a space that she shouldn't intrude upon. She was also a little bit worried about what she might see if she did take a peek.

Gren rolled over as her mind started to slow down. Sleeping on the sand was annoying but in a strange way it was comfortable. She knew that they would be rescued eventually, even if she couldn't contact the Learning Center, and her mind drifted to the happy time when a water craft would approach and they would realize that they were headed home. In the micro before she fell asleep there was a movement that didn't quite make sense to her, but her brain ignored it and allowed her to rest. Soon her own private dreams formed in her mind.

Tayo was the first one to wake up. She decided to walk down by the water for a few hundreds. She stayed where she could see everyone, and where they could see her once they were awake. She stared long and hard at the ocean in front of her. It was gorgeous. She was surprised that she wasn't more worried about their predicament. Dod was right, their path was one that shouldn't be difficult to trace. It might take a few rotations, but she knew that they would be rescued, even if they weren't able to contact the Learning Center through wandering.

"It's beautiful, isn't it?" Tayo was startled, she hadn't heard Sham approaching. "Sorry, didn't mean to scare you."

"That's okay. I didn't realize that anyone else was awake."

"How do we get ourselves into these situations?" Sham asked.

"I don't know. Not all Wanderers have these problems. Grey told me once that his life is pretty boring, compared to what we've been through. Of course, he doesn't know what happened two orbits ago at the Learning Center, but he knows that something did happen. He respects that I can't talk about it."

Sham shook his head. "Do we really have to talk about Grey? What's going on with the two of you, anyway?"

"We're..." Tayo searched for the right word, "exploring." She immediately realized that it wasn't the word that she was looking for. "We're getting to know each other. We're dating, for lack of a better word, but we're taking things slowly. Grey has been hurt a lot in his life and he has a hard time trusting. I respect that. He's a good guy, Sham, you really should give him a chance."

"Exploring?" Sham picked the one word that Tayo regretted saying. "Wow, that sounds like a great word for a relationship. Tayo, my friend, you know that you can do a lot better than Grey."

"Grey treats me like I'm the most special person on Terra," Tayo said. "I like his company. I'm still young, I have another orbit as an Apprentice, and then I have a career to think about. I'm in no hurry to get joined or anything like that, and Grey isn't either. What we have works for both of us."

"Joined? You'd better not be thinking about getting joined, especially to Grey!"

Tayo laughed. "Sham, Grey and I aren't getting joined. And if we were, it wouldn't be any of your business."

"He's too old for you anyway."

"He's two orbits older than I am. Not a big deal. And since when have you gone all parental on me?"

Sham grinned. "After all that we've been through, we're family. For a long time now I've thought that you and Gren are almost like my sisters."

"Only Gren and me?" Tayo asked. "What about Calli?"

"Why, what has she said? Have you talked to Calli alone?"

"Not much. Why, should I?"

Sham grinned again. "Just wondering."

"Sham, Tayo!" Lawson's voice yelled. "Get back up here. Now!"

"Sounds like we're being summoned," Sham said.

It didn't take long for Sham and Tayo to rejoin their friends. Immediately they could see that something was wrong. "What's going on?" Sham asked.

Lawson pointed to where they kept their supplies. "The food is gone."

"It was probably taken by an animal or something," Sham

commented. "We found some edible plants, we'll be fine. Calli even tried one and she survived."

"It wasn't an animal," Dod commented. He was staring at something on the ground near where their food used to be. "Look, footprints. They're human."

Chapter Nineteen

Dod was right, there was a set of what appeared to be human footprints near where the food used to be. The group could track them to a grassy area that wasn't too far away. The footprints were on the small side, and the person who made them hadn't been wearing shoes. "I'm so stupid," Gren said at last. "I thought I saw something last night, I got a glimpse of movement, but I was tired and I went to sleep without giving it any thought."

Lawson glanced at Gren. "The last thing that you are is stupid. Can you remember anything about what you saw?"

Gren shook her head. "No, all that I remember is that there was some movement that didn't seem quite right."

"Well, we now know we're not alone," Titus said. "I doubt that this person means us any harm. If he had bad intentions, he could have attacked us while we slept. He waited, and then just took our food."

"Or she," Calli added. "The footprints aren't that big."

"He's hurt," Dod said. He was staring at the ground near where the footprints ended. "Look, there's blood here. There are a couple more drops along the way."

"Maybe we should find him," Lawson said. "After all, he's barefoot, wounded, and hungry enough to take our food."

"Speaking of food," Angel said, "what are we going to do?"

"That's simple," Titus replied. "We found some when we got here. We'll just gather what we need."

"How about we break up into three groups?" Lawson suggested.

Gren took over. "Great idea. Titus and Sham, you know where

the food that you found is located, so you're in charge of that. Lawson and I will look around, see if we can figure out who this mysterious person is. Chances are that he or she needs to be rescued as well. Calli, Tayo, Angel, and Dod, you all stay here and watch over our other supplies. We don't want to lose anything else." Gren needed to talk to Lawson alone, and the situation would allow her the opportunity to do just that.

"But..." Dod protested.

Lawson interrupted. "Dod, we need you to use your investigative skills and see if you can come up with any more clues. You've been a huge help already. Angel will look with you, right Angel?" The young Purple nodded. "Good. Let's give it, um, two units. We can then meet back here."

Everyone agreed to the plan. As Sham and Titus started to walk away Lawson called after them. "Sham! Don't forget the analyzer!" Sham ran back and picked up the tool. He flashed a quick smile at Calli before he rejoined his former partner.

As Angel and Dod looked in the grassy area for more clues, Calli and Tayo sat down in the sand not too far away. They could see the Purples but they were far enough away so that they could have a private conversation. "Okay, Calli," Tayo started, "what's going on between you and Sham?"

Calli looked away, slightly embarrassed. "Do you think that Sham and I have an 'it'?"

"A what?"

"An 'it'," Calli repeated. She made quotation marks with her fingers. "You know, kind of like the thing that Gren and Lawson have and can't do anything about. Sham thinks that we have an 'it' and I'm not sure what to think."

Tayo grinned. "Oh, now I understand. When we were near the water earlier, I had no idea what Sham was talking about."

"Why, what did he say?"

"Not much," Tayo answered. "He just wanted to know if you and I had talked at all. He didn't have a chance to say much more because Lawson called us. Why, what happened?"

"Nothing, really." Calli started to scribble in the sand with her finger. "We were talking about Gren and Lawson. He kept referring to that thing that they have as 'it' and he said how they're going to have to deal with 'it' eventually. He then said that he and I are soon going to have to deal with our own 'it' as well. I didn't know that we had one."

"You didn't realize that Sham has a thing for you? Come on, Calli, I'm sure that even Angel and Dod have figured that out. The question is, how do you feel about him?"

"I...I haven't really thought all that much about it. I mean, I always thought that it was just Sham being Sham. He doesn't take anything seriously, I'm not sure what is different about this."

"Sham is taking this seriously," Tayo pointed out. "At least more seriously than most things. And you didn't answer my question. How do you feel about Sham?"

Calli stood up and brushed off the extra sand. "Let's go check on Angel and Dod. Maybe they've found something else interesting."

Gren waited for the right micro as she and Lawson searched. She had something to tell Lawson and it was important. She was grateful to have a little bit of time alone with him. They rounded a group of trees and ended up at the watering hole. Since the tension had grown thick the last time that they were at that location, Gren figured that she had finally found the right micro. "Lawson?"

Lawson was looking at the spot where they had almost kissed. The pain was still there, but he felt better because he had let Gren know how he felt. "I didn't purposely come here," he said. "I was just looking for clues as to who took our food. I guess I didn't pay close enough attention to our path."

"Lawson..."

"Let's just keep going." He took a step in front of Gren.

"Lawson!" Gren grabbed him by the shoulders and turned him around. Without giving herself a chance to think about what she was doing, she kissed him. Orbits worth of tension and waiting melted away as they both got lost in the micro. After a hundred Gren pulled away. "I've made up my mind, Lawson," she said softly. "I want us to be together. We still can't be, not yet, not until after we're licensed. But I can't imagine my life without you."

Lawson couldn't help but smile. "What if Haas offers both of us Associate positions?"

"Then I'll turn him down and work somewhere else. I've been a fool, Lawson, putting everything else in front of you. I'm not going to do that any longer. I'm done making excuses."

"You don't know how scared I was that I would never hear those words." Lawson moved closer, hoping for another kiss.

Gren put up her hand and stopped him. "Sorry, but we still need to follow the rules. We both work for Haas, so things need to continue the way that they have been, at least until after the Trials."

"Just one more kiss?" Lawson pleaded.

Gren kissed Lawson on the cheek. "That's going to have to hold you. Now let's go, we need to keep searching for the person who took our food." She took his hand and started to walk forward.

Lawson walked by Gren's side, trying to remember what it was that they were searching for.

· · ●●●●· ·

Titus and Sham arrived where they had found the edible plants. Sham immediately started to analyze things, just to make sure that they were still safe. Titus sat down on a rock. "Hey," Sham said, "I'm not going to do all the work by myself."

"Just give me a hundred to try to reach the Learning Center."

"When did you get to be such an expert on wandering distances?" Sham asked.

"I'm not. But just let me try, okay?" Titus got comfortable and closed his eyes.

To Sham, it looked more like Titus was dreaming than trying to wander. He didn't think much of it at first, every Dream Wanderer had a different style. He continued to analyze the plants that looked suitable for eating.

"So, it's not part of the plan?" Titus said out loud.

Sham looked at his friend. He was sitting the same way, nothing had changed. He still appeared to be dreaming. A few micros later Titus opened his eyes again. "Any luck?" Sham asked.

"I wasn't able to wander the Learning Center," Titus said. "I didn't even find any traces of tonic."

"I have one question," Sham said. "Who was wandering you? And what 'plan' were you talking about?"

Chapter Twenty

Titus looked at Sham and thought for a micro. He had to figure out how to handle the situation. He decided to play dumb. "What are you talking about?" he asked at last. "And, by the way, that was two questions."

Sham rolled his eyes. "Titus, I've seen you wander thousands of times. What you just did is not your personal style. I've also been wandering your dreams for just short of forever. I know what you're like when someone is wandering you. One thing that you almost always do is to speak out loud when you're being wandered. At first I thought that maybe you were talking to Gren. Is that it? Do the two of you have some sort of plan cooked up? If so, why are you keeping it a secret?"

"Gren wasn't wandering me," Titus said with a sigh. "It was Ladinda."

"Ladinda!" Sham was excited. "So, we're going to get out of here soon! Titus, why didn't you tell me?"

"We're here for a couple more rotations," Titus said. "She said something about having a hard time securing a water craft."

Sham looked disappointed. "Oh. Well, let's go tell the others. They're going to be thrilled."

Titus jumped to his feet and grabbed Sham's arm. "No, wait! You can't do that."

"Why not?" When Titus didn't answer right away, Sham remembered what he had heard his former partner say during the dream. "What 'plan' were you referring to when Ladinda was wandering you?"

"You can't tell anyone," Titus said. He glanced around. He

knew that they were alone, but he still wanted to make sure. "This entire trip has been one of Ladinda's tests. She set everything up so that Angel and Dod would have to start working together as a team. And it's worked, they're finally getting along. Ladinda thinks that they need a little more time away from the Learning Center. She doesn't want them to be able to easily revert to their old ways. This trip needs to change them."

"This whole thing was faked?" Sham asked.

Titus nodded. "Ladinda told me her plan when she asked me to stay behind. You remember, when she gave me the book for Cassidy. Ward fixed the fuel cell so that it would fail. I knew exactly where we needed to end up. Ladinda has known where we are the whole time. I've been sneaking off and letting her wander. That's what I was doing when you caught me that other time, when I told you to go bother Calli. I also knew that I needed to talk to Ladinda now. This is one of our set times, and I thought that I could fake that I was trying to wander. I guess I was wrong."

"So, what about all of us? Why are we here?"

"With Gren and Lawson, it's obvious," Titus explained. "They're supposed to show Angel and Dod that a male/female partnering can work. Calli and Tayo are here because of the problems that they had in the past. Ladinda thought that they might be able to use their former animosity to help Angel and Dod work through their own problems. Ladinda also somehow knew that I have a water craft license. That woman seems to know everything."

Sham stared at Titus for a micro. "So, why am I here?"

"To flirt with Calli?" Titus suggested, trying to lighten the mood. The look on Sham's face told Titus that it hadn't worked.

"Look, who knows why Ladinda does anything? All I know is that she has her reasons. And her plan seems to be working, because Angel and Dod are bonding."

"That's true. So, what about the person who stole our food? What did Ladinda have to say about that?"

"That was what you heard me talking about. It wasn't part of the plan. Ladinda doesn't think that it's anything to worry about. She said that as long as we keep using the partner system, we shouldn't have any problems."

"Because Ladinda knows everything."

"So, you won't say anything?"

Sham thought for a micro. "I'll keep your secret, for now. But I think that we need to tell everyone that you've made contact with the Learning Center."

"Sham, we can't do that. Ladinda doesn't want anyone to know that contact has been made. They're even taking a break from wandering back there, that's why Gren can't find any traces of tonic. The entire Learning Center is doing things differently for this to work. Ladinda said that she'll tell me when or if I can say anything."

"And what Ladinda says goes."

Titus nodded. "Sham, do you know any Wanderer who has more influence than she does? The woman even talked Haas into taking Apprentices for the first time in decades! If we mess this up and don't follow her plan, we'll never be able to get a job with a reputable practice after we pass the Trials. We'll be blacklisted. That's if we pass the Trials. Who knows if Ladinda has any say as far as they are concerned."

"The Trials," Sham repeated. "I haven't thought of those since we arrived here."

"That's the other part of Ladinda's plan," Titus said. "She knows how much pressure all four of us are under. She thought that this would be a good way to get our minds off of the Trials for a little while. She's especially worried about Gren, and in a strange way this has been good for her."

"Yeah, she and Lawson are fighting about other things instead."

Titus smiled. "Exactly. So...can I trust you to keep this to yourself?"

Sham thought for several micros. "You know that you can. But I'm not sure why we let Ladinda keep manipulating us like this."

"We need to get some food," Titus said. "I'm sure that everyone is starving by now. Ladinda did know that there's plenty of food and clean water here on this island. She wanted to make sure that we had everything that we would need."

"Of course, she did."

The two friends worked side by side and gathered what they hoped would be enough food for everyone. Titus was slightly relieved that he had been able to share his secret with someone. He was sure that Sham would keep it for him.

"Let's head back to camp," Sham said eventually. "Can't let everyone stay hungry."

"Everyone, or Calli?" Titus teased. "What's going on between the two of you?"

Sham grinned. "Nothing much. Just destiny."

Chapter Twenty-One

By the end of the rotation the group was no closer to discovering who had taken their food than they had been that morning. Everyone sat around the fire to try to figure out what to do next. They had made a meal but they all just picked at it. Calli was the only one who had tried the food earlier, and she had warned the others about how bad it was. Gren and Lawson sat close to each other, obviously getting along. Gren was still frustrated because she had been unable to contact the Learning Center, but her mood in general had improved. Sham and Calli sat on opposite sides of the fire. Calli would glance at Sham from time to time, and he would immediately wink at her. Angel and Dod sat next to each other. No one mentioned how well the two Purples were getting along, but they all noticed.

"Anyone have any ideas on how we should handle this tonight?" Tayo asked. "The mystery person did wait until he thought that we were all asleep last night."

"We'll keep watch," Titus suggested. "One person will stay awake at all times. If that person gets tired, he or she will wake up the next one in line. We'll all take turns, except for Angel and Dod."

"We want to help too!" Dod exclaimed. Angel nodded in agreement.

"You can be the final two," Gren said quickly. "You can work together." She shot a look to all her friends, and she could tell that none of them had any intention of waking Angel or Dod up.

"I doubt he's going to be back, anyway," Sham said. He put down his plate, there was still food on it. "The only reason he stole our food was because the stuff on this island is terrible." No one argued with him.

"What order should we keep watch in?" Calli asked.

"I'll stay up first," Gren said. "I'm not tired at all, and I want to try to reach the Learning Center."

"They never use tonic this late," Lawson pointed out.

"You never know," Gren said. "Something is off, I should have been able to find them by now. I need to keep trying."

Sham glanced quickly at Titus. They both knew exactly what was off.

"Wake me up when you get tired," Lawson said. "I'll take the second shift."

"I'll go third," Calli said quickly.

"I call fourth," Sham chimed in.

"You want fifth or sixth?" Titus asked Tayo.

"You take fifth, I'm an early riser." Tayo glanced at Angel and Dod. "And then you two can watch after me." She had no intention of waking them up.

The group cleaned up and put away their plates and other cooking supplies. They were glad that the mysterious person had left those alone. There was still plenty of uncooked food left, they would not have to gather more in the morning. After the fire died down they decided that everyone except for Gren should try to get some sleep. She sat by herself, close to the girls' sleeping area. The temperature was comfortable, but the wind was picking up. Gren closed her eyes and tried to reach out. She couldn't find anything.

⋅ ∘ ∘●◉●∘ ∘

Calli was sound asleep when Lawson woke her up. From the light of the stars she could tell that he was exhausted. "I've got it from here," she said as she sat up.

"Thanks." Lawson took a few steps towards the area where the guys were all sleeping. "It's been quiet. Remember, when you get tired, Sham's turn to watch is next."

"Got it." She paused for half a micro. "So, Lawson, is everything okay with you and Gren?"

Lawson grinned, and even in the darkness Calli could see it. "Never better."

"That's good to hear. Now go get some rest."

After Lawson had joined the guys, Calli stood up and walked away from where the rest of the girls were sleeping. There wasn't a lot of light, but she could still see the ocean. The sound of the waves was calming, and she knew that she needed to do something if she wanted to stay awake. If she fell asleep on her watch Sham would never let her live it down. Sham. She didn't want to think about him. Since she was tired, she was scared of where those thoughts would take her.

Calli decided instead to concentrate on the mysterious person who had taken their food. Who was he? Was he stranded as well, or did he want to live alone on the island? Was he alone? Why was there blood in the footprints? She thought that maybe Sham was right, maybe the poor person just wanted some better tasting food. What they had made for the evening meal had tasted pretty bad.

"Even Sham didn't finish his, and I thought that he would eat anything," Calli said out loud. She shook her head. She didn't want to think about him. She turned her thoughts again to the other person on the island. Would he want to be rescued when someone from the Learning Center finally figured out where they were? They needed to try harder to learn who the person was. He might need help. Calli remembered her extra blanket, and decided to leave that near where the rest of their supplies were. Maybe the stranded person would take the blanket, and they would be able to talk to him and find out what was going on. She doubted that they were in any danger. If the person wanted to hurt them, he would have when he took the food.

Calli placed the blanket where it could be seen from several different places. She then decided to sit near where the girls slept for a while. She didn't want to scare the person away. A couple of times she thought that she saw something, but then realized that the blanket was just moving in the wind.

Calli sat there for over a unit and nothing happened. Eventually the sound of the waves got to her, and she decided that it was time to wake up Sham. She knew that she couldn't keep her eyes open much longer. She got up, not really wanting to do what she was about to do. As she walked to where the guys were, she could see that Sham was lying on his left side. Calli walked behind him and gently shook his right shoulder. "Sham?" she whispered. He didn't move. She shook his shoulder again, slightly harder. "Sham. It's your turn to keep watch."

It took Sham a micro to realize what was going on. "Calli," he said quietly. "I was just dreaming about you."

"It's your turn to keep watch."

"That's not what you said in my dream."

Calli rolled her eyes. "I placed an extra blanket with the supplies. I thought that maybe the person who took our food might want a blanket as well. He probably needs our help."

Sham stretched and yawned. "Good idea." He kept his voice down so as to not wake the others. "Have you given any more thought to what we talked about before?"

"Sham, right now I'm too tired to think about anything."

"Fair enough. You go get some sleep. But promise me that we'll talk tomorrow morning."

Calli waited for a micro and then nodded. "I promise."

In the dim light Sham's smile was still heartwarming. "Until tomorrow, then. Good night, dear Calli."

Calli sighed and shook her head as she walked away. "Good night, Sham."

After Calli was out of sight Sham lay on his back and stared at the stars. His life was close to perfect. He knew that they weren't in any real danger and that the whole situation had been manipulated by Ladinda, so he realized that they had nothing to worry about. He would soon be an officially licensed Dream Wanderer. He could continue to work for Cassidy if he wanted to, which was an exciting prospect to him. He really enjoyed everything about her practice; with the exception of Grey. He had a great glidemobile. The best part of his life was that the girl that he had been interested in for a long time finally seemed to be interested in him as well. He wasn't even worried about the Trials at that micro. He couldn't imagine being happier, unless of course the conversation with Calli went the way that he hoped that it would go. That would make him beyond happy. Sham stared at the stars and his mind started to drift.

· · ●●◯● · ·

"Calli? Calli!" The sound of Tayo calling at the top of her lungs woke everyone else.

"What's going on?" Gren asked. She wiped the sleep out of her eyes.

"I can't find Calli," Tayo said with panic in her voice.

Lawson made it over to where the girls had been sleeping. "She's got to be around here somewhere. She was fine when I had her relieve me last night."

"No one ever woke me up," Tayo said.

"Me neither," Titus said as he, Sham, and Dod joined everyone else.

Sham realized what had happened. "I...I...I must have fallen asleep."

"Don't worry about that, we were all tired," Gren said. "Falling asleep doesn't have anything to do with Calli."

"She said something about leaving an extra blanket with the supplies," Sham remembered. "She thought that whoever took the food might take the blanket, and then we could find out who this person is."

"Let's go check," Gren suggested. "Everyone else, just keep calling her. She's got to be around here somewhere."

Sham, Gren, and Titus all walked to where they kept the supplies. The blanket was gone.

Chapter Twenty-Two

As soon as Sham realized that the blanket was missing, he grabbed Titus by the shoulders. "Where is she? What happened to her?"

"Sham, how am I supposed to know? You're the one who fell asleep."

"So, this is all my fault?" Sham let go of Titus' shoulders and paused for only a micro before he punched him in the jaw. "What, you're telling me that this isn't a part of your plan?"

Titus hoped that Gren didn't hear. "Sham, be quiet. I have no idea what happened to Calli. And you better not even think of hitting me again."

As if challenged, Sham swung. This time Titus blocked it and hit back. Soon they were both on the ground.

"Enough!" Gren screamed. "This isn't doing Calli any good. We need to look around, see if we can find some clues." When the roommates didn't listen, Gren bent down and grabbed hold of Sham's arm as he pulled it back. He was on top of Titus and had just hit him in the face. "Stop! Calli wouldn't want this."

Sham stood up and took a few steps away from Titus. Gren placed herself between them so that they couldn't start fighting again. "You don't know the whole story, Gren."

Titus, who was sitting on the ground dabbing the blood that was near his mouth, stared hard at his former partner. "Sham, we talked about this. Don't. You promised."

"That was before my girlfriend disappeared."

"Girlfriend?" Titus repeated. "Calli's not your girlfriend."

"She was going to be. She promised me that we'd talk this

morning. But then you and your stupid plan ruined everything."

"What plan?" Gren asked. "That's the second time that you mentioned it. What's going on?"

Titus shot another harsh look at Sham. "Don't."

Sham ignored the warning. "This whole thing is a setup. All planned by Ladinda, to get Angel and Dod alone so that they would have to rely on each other. Titus has been in on it the whole time."

Gren shook her head, letting the words sink in. "She did it to me again," she mumbled.

"Gren," Titus said quickly, "you can't tell anyone else. Ladinda didn't even want Sham to know, but he caught me when she was wandering me. I had to tell him the truth."

"That's why you haven't been able to find Hutch," Sham continued. "They're not using tonic right now at the Learning Center. They know exactly where we are, but Ladinda won't send someone to get us."

"Why not?" Gren asked.

"Who knows why Ladinda does what she does?" Titus replied. "She told me that Angel and Dod need more time."

"Can you make contact with her now?" Gren asked. "Maybe she knows where Calli is."

"It's earlier than our first normal scheduled time, but I'll try." Titus sat up and closed his eyes.

Gren walked over and stood next to Sham. She didn't want to get in Titus' way. In the distance she could hear Calli's name being called. "Are you okay? I don't think I've ever seen you two go at it like that before."

Sham turned and looked at Gren. "I'm fine."

"No you're not." There was a large gash next to Sham's right eye, and it was bleeding. "Let me take a look at that." Gren touched the cut and Sham flinched. "I think there are some bandages in the emergency supplies. That is, unless those are gone too."

"I'm fine," Sham repeated. "He only got in one good punch."

Gren ignored him and opened one of the containers. She took out a bandage and then approached Sham again. "Stand still. Let me get this for you." Gren reached up and gently placed the bandage on Sham's face.

"What's going on here?" Neither of them had heard Lawson approaching.

"Lawson," Gren said with a start. "I didn't know that you were there."

"I can see that. Since when are you two so chummy?"

"Chummy?" Sham repeated.

"Sham's hurt and I was placing a bandage on his cut," Gren explained. "That's all."

"So, I wait orbits until I can even take your hand, and then I find you over here like this with Sham?" A vision of a dream from two orbits earlier flashed in Lawson's mind. It was a dream that Hutch had manipulated, and it had involved Sham and Gren. He couldn't quite forget the images from the dream, no matter how hard he tried. He had never told Gren the details of the session, but she knew that something had happened that rotation.

"Lawson, where is this coming from?"

"How did you even get hurt, Sham? I thought you were just coming over here to check the supplies."

"I got into a fight with my former best friend," Sham said. "Since this is all his fault."

"This is Titus' fault?" Lawson asked. "Why?"

Gren knew that Ladinda wanted as few people as possible to

know about the plan. "Calli left a blanket out over here, to see if the person who took our food might want that as well. The blanket is gone. It all has to be related somehow."

Titus, who had been in a dream-like state and didn't realize that Lawson was there, opened his eyes. "No luck," he said.

"No luck with what?" Lawson asked.

"Titus was trying to wander," Gren explained.

"Why was Titus trying to wander?" Lawson asked. "We all know that you're the best at finding someone. If anyone can find Calli through wandering, it's you, Gren. Something is not making sense here."

"If I tried to wander, these two might have tried to kill each other again," Gren said. "You weren't here, Lawson. I've never seen them act like that before." She smiled at Lawson, hoping to soften his mood. "And since when have our lives made sense?"

Lawson sighed. "Good point," he conceded. "I'm sorry, I don't know what got into me."

"Now," Gren continued, "let's look and see if we can figure anything out. Maybe we can find more footprints or something."

It didn't take long to spot a couple of clues. There were more footprints that were similar to the ones that they had noticed when their food went missing, but they didn't have blood in them. There was a set of footprints made by shoes that were not too far from them. "They look like they could be Calli's size," Lawson commented.

"But they could be from when she left the blanket," Gren reminded him.

The set of bare footprints led off into the woods. The other set was harder to follow because they weren't clear. They suddenly stopped.

Something else caught Gren's attention. There was an object in one of the bushes that was on the edge of the beach and the woods. "What's that?" she said. She walked over to it, making sure that there were no footprints to disturb. She took the object off of the bush. "It's cloth."

"Let me see." Sham took the cloth from Gren. "It's Calli's. It's a piece of her shirt."

Chapter Twenty-Three

When they could find no other signs of Calli, everyone else gathered by the fire pit to come up with a plan. They didn't bother to make a fire, no one was hungry. It was decided that Tayo would stay on the beach with Angel and Dod. The two Purples started to protest, but then Gren explained that they could practice getting into a dream-like state and then maybe Calli would make contact with one of them. Once they realized that they could do something important by staying put, they agreed to do their part. Tayo would spend her time trying to wander. Since she and Calli were so close, if anyone knew what to look for, it was Tayo.

"So, Sham, Titus, Gren, and I will all go search," Lawson said. "Normal pairings?"

"No," Gren said quickly. "Why don't you look with Titus and I'll search with Sham." Gren really wanted to go with Titus to find out more about Ladinda's plan, but she knew that she couldn't trust Sham to keep it a secret. She wasn't sure why she didn't want anyone else to know, except for the fact that Ladinda always had things under control and always had her reasons.

"Fine with me," Sham replied. "I want to spend as little time with him as possible."

"I don't want to work with you either." Titus rubbed his face. He hadn't been hurt badly in the fight, he had a couple of small cuts and a bruise on his jaw. Sham looked worse than Titus did.

"Yeah, you're scared of what I'd do to you."

Titus laughed. "Are you kidding? Even Grey hits harder than you do, and he hit me by accident!"

"Stop it!" Tayo screamed. "This isn't doing Calli any good. We need to start doing something to try to find her."

"We should eat something before we go," Gren said, standing up. "We don't need to cook anything; we'll just eat it raw. We're going to need our energy, and we might not be back here for a while."

"I'll get it with you," Lawson said. He waited until they were fairly far away from everyone else and then lowered his voice. "What's going on?"

"Titus implied that it's Sham's fault that Calli is missing because he fell asleep," Gren explained. She purposely left out all about Ladinda and her plan.

"So, they fought?" Lawson asked. "That's not like them."

"In case you never noticed, Sham's got a thing for Calli," Gren said. "Apparently they were supposed to talk about their feelings this morning, try to figure things out." Gren smiled at Lawson. "There seems to be a lot of that going around."

"I'm sorry about before. I saw you with Sham, and I thought, well, I don't know what I thought."

Gren laughed. "The last person that you need to be worried about is Sham."

"So, who should I be worried about?"

Gren picked up some of the food and handed it to Lawson. "Here, make yourself useful."

After they all ate something Titus excused himself for a couple of hundreds. Gren was pretty sure that he was going to try to contact Ladinda. She wanted to follow, but since everyone else assumed that he was going to the necessary area she knew that she couldn't. When he returned, he shook his head slightly, letting Gren know that he hadn't made contact. They then decided to begin the search. Gren and Sham started near where they had discovered the torn piece of cloth. Titus and Lawson went in a different direction. Tayo, Angel, and Dod all stayed behind. Tayo tried to wander, while Angel and Dod let their minds drift. They all planned to communicate by wandering from time to time. It was a routine that the former students all knew too well.

∘ ∘ ●◗◖● ∘ ∘

Gren wasn't going to tell Sham that she would rather be with either Lawson or Titus. He was unusually quiet as they walked. "How's your eye feeling?" she asked at last.

"I'll survive," Sham answered. "Look, Gren, I realize that the reason that you didn't want me to search with Lawson is because I'd tell him about Ladinda's plan. And you're right, I would have."

"You want to find Calli," Gren said. "I do too. So, what's going on with the two of you? She's been kind of distant lately."

"She's finally realized how awesome I am," Sham replied. He paused. "Actually, I've finally realized how awesome she is. And now she's missing."

"Sham, we've been in worse situations than this," Gren said. "Our final orbit, this is how it all started. We found a piece of cloth, remember?"

"You think that this is still a setup by Ladinda?" Sham asked.

"I don't know what to think."

Sham thought for a micro. "Maybe it is. But we still need to treat this like Calli is in real danger. We can't take any chances."

"I agree."

Sham paused again. "Titus is right. This is all my fault. If I hadn't fallen asleep..."

"There's nothing that you can do about that," Gren said. "We need to concentrate on finding her, not on things that we could have done differently."

"I know, but still..." Sham tilted his head back and took a deep breath. "CALLI!!!" he called as loudly as he could.

"You and Gren suddenly seem to be getting along better than ever," Titus remarked. The last thing that he wanted was for Lawson to ask him why he and Sham had fought, so he thought that bringing up Gren was a good idea.

Lawson grinned. "Yeah. We talked. We finally talked about everything that we had been avoiding."

"I take it that you're happy with how the conversation turned out?"

"Happy?" Lawson laughed. "She kissed me."

"Gren kissed you? Wouldn't that mean that she had to break Haas' rule?"

"Yup. But she did it anyway. Gren and I might have a future together after all, my friend."

"What if Haas offers both of you a job?" Titus asked. "Wouldn't the same old rules then still be in place?"

"That's one of the things that we talked about. Gren told me that she'd rather be with me than work for Haas. Can you believe that?"

"It's about time."

Off in the distance Sham could be heard calling Calli's name.

"What's going on with you and Sham?" Lawson asked.

Titus wasn't quite sure how to respond. "He's, well, he's upset about Calli, and taking it out on me."

"Gren said that you told him it was his fault because he fell asleep. That's why he's so mad at you."

Titus quietly breathed a sigh of relief. Gren had given him the excuse that he was looking for. "Yeah, I said that. It was totally uncalled for, I know. It's just, I don't know, maybe I've been a little bit jealous."

"You have a thing for Calli?"

"No!" Titus exclaimed right away. "We're friends, that's all. It's just that you and Gren have each other, you always have. Sham and Calli now have each other. Tayo and Grey are dating. That leaves me alone. I'd like to have someone special in my future as well."

Lawson put a hand on his friend's shoulder. "It will happen, Titus. There's someone perfect out there for you. Just be patient, and don't settle. Hey, how about Aribella? I don't think she's seeing anyone right now."

"Yeah, and she's also old enough to be my mother!"

"No she's not." Lawson laughed. "Your mother's younger sister, maybe, but not your mother."

Every few steps Sham would call out Calli's name. He would then listen for a response that didn't come. Once a unit Gren would try to reach out to Tayo and Lawson. She was a bit discouraged that there was no new information. The only good news was that Tayo had Angel and Dod practicing their wandering skills. They had both been able to enter the other's dream. That proved that they had started to trust each other. After what Sham had told her, Gren didn't even bother trying to contact the Learning Center.

Once it started to get late Gren suggested that they head back to camp. "We're not going to be able to find Calli in the dark, and we don't want to get lost as well." Sham reluctantly agreed.

◦ ◦ ●●◐ ◦ ◦

Tayo had fixed some food, and they ate mostly in silence. At one point Titus mentioned that he hadn't had any luck wandering all rotation. Only Sham and Gren knew that he meant that he hadn't been in contact with Ladinda.

Once it was time to get some sleep, they decided to again take turns keeping watch. Sham moved up one spot and said that he would take over at Calli's turn. He was not going to make the same mistake and sleep through his shift again.

Chapter Twenty-Four

"Holy splarsh, it happened again!" The sound of Titus' loud exclamation woke everyone else up.

"What happened again?" Lawson asked as he sat up and stretched.

"Sham didn't wake me up," Titus said. "And he's not here."

Gren was the first female to approach the guys. "What's going on?"

"Sham isn't here," Titus explained. "Gren, sorry about the expression. I know it's not your favorite."

"Apology accepted, but next time remember that there are children here," she said. "Now, what's going on with Sham?"

"He didn't wake me up again," Titus explained. "And he's not here."

Tayo and Angel joined the others. "Maybe he's just, you know..." Tayo suggested.

"I'll go check." Lawson jumped to his feet and ran over to the secluded spot that they had designated as the necessary area for the guys. "Nope," he called back loudly.

"I'll check the supplies, see if anything is missing," Gren said. Everyone else scattered and started calling Sham's name. When Gren reached the supply area, she waved for the others else to join her. Once they were all there she said, "He's fine, he's looking for Calli."

"How do you know?" Titus asked.

Gren pointed at the ground. In the sand the words, "I'm fine, I'm looking for Calli," were clearly written.

Sham walked for units before he stopped to rest. He figured that since the mysterious person had only shown up at night, the night was probably the best time to search for Calli. They still didn't know for sure whether or not the person had anything to do with her disappearance, but he decided to assume that the two were related. He was determined to find Calli, no matter what. He had brought some water with him because he didn't want to take time out of his search to look for it. He had also grabbed some food before he left. He had one of the analyzers with him as well. He knew that Calli would need food and water when he found her, and since he didn't want to carry too much, he needed to make sure that anything that he found along the way was safe. Sham hiked for a long time after the sun rose. He didn't take a break until he was so tired that he couldn't go on.

"Well," Lawson said, "he took a bag, one of the analyzers and some water. Maybe some food, I don't know how much we had. It looks like everything else is untouched."

"I don't know what he thinks he's going to prove," Titus added. "We need to stick together. We've said ever since we arrived here that no one was to go off alone."

"That all changed when Calli disappeared," Gren commented. "Sham's obviously not thinking straight right now."

"So, now what?" Tayo asked. "We go looking for both Sham and Calli? I mean, how long is this going to go on? Who is going to disappear next?"

"No one else is going to disappear," Titus said. There was an authoritative tone in his voice. "Back at the Learning Center they must have figured out where we are by now. All they have to do is to send someone to find us."

Gren looked at Titus, hoping that he was letting her know that he had been in contact with Ladinda. Titus shook his head slightly, informing her that no contact had been made.

"Well," Lawson said at last, "we obviously have to rethink our groups. How are we going to do this?"

"Same as before, I guess," Gren said. "I'll just join you and Titus."

"So, Dod and I are stuck back here again?" Angel asked.

"You're not stuck," Gren explained. "We need someone to stay here and to keep watch over what we have left. Plus we always have to have someone either wandering or ready to be wandered. It's the best way to communicate."

"I still think that there's more that we could do," Dod said.

"I was going to say that!" Angel smiled at her partner. At least Ladinda's plan had worked on one level.

Sham didn't sleep long. He gave his body a chance to recharge, and then he was ready to go on. He took a bite of one of the root vegetables that they had found. "This stuff is terrible," he said to the air. "I can't wait until we're finally back home and we can have decent food again. I think I'll take Calli to a nice restaurant for our first real date, maybe one of the places that Winnie liked so much when she visited last orbit." Sham took another bite of the vegetable and washed it down with some water. "CALLI!!!!!!"

∘ ∘ ●◐◑ ∘ ∘

A unit after they started searching, Gren, Lawson, and Titus took a break to try to wander. Gren searched for a sign of Calli or Sham, Lawson was unsuccessful in contacting Tayo, and Titus sat on the side, away from the others. Gren knew what Titus was trying to do but Lawson had no idea. Both Gren and Lawson were finished before Titus was. "He looks more like he's trying to be wandered than that he's trying to wander," Lawson pointed out.

Gren shrugged. She hated not letting Lawson know the whole truth, but also knew that she shouldn't. "Maybe he's hoping that Sham will find him. Sham has to be looking for Calli, he might enter Titus' dream instead."

"I wouldn't want to be a part of that dream," Lawson commented.

"I wouldn't want to be sharing a dwelling with the two of them once we finally get home."

Lawson sighed. "Yeah, it's going to be interesting. Maybe I should look for a place of my own."

"It might be a good idea to wait until after the Trials before you add the stress of moving to your life," Gren suggested.

"The Trials. I've hardly thought about them since we got here."

Gren nodded. "I know what you mean. Just a few rotations ago I couldn't think about anything but the Trials, and now they're somewhere in the back of my mind." She noticed that Titus had changed his body position, meaning that he was no longer in a dream-like state. "Any luck, Titus? Were either Sham or Calli able to wander you?"

Titus looked confused for a micro, then realized what Gren meant. "No. No one wandered me."

"Let's keep looking," Lawson suggested. He put out a hand

and helped Titus to his feet.

"Good idea," Gren said. She glanced at Titus. "It's funny how people have distinct styles when they wander. Lawson and I both picked up right away that you were trying to let someone wander, instead of trying to wander yourself." Gren squinted her eyes in thought for a micro. "Did that make sense?"

Titus smiled. He knew exactly what Gren meant. "Yeah, I know what you're saying."

Lawson laughed. "I'm glad that you do. For a micro I was trying to figure out how you could wander your own dream."

· ○ ◐ ● ◑ ○ ·

Sham mumbled to himself as he walked. He hated nature with everything in him, and couldn't wait until he was back home, indoors at his dwelling. He knew that it might be a problem to continue to share a place with Titus, but he figured that he could deal with that later. He was mad at Titus, but he realized that deep down it was Ladinda who truly angered him. "Her stupid plans," he said out loud. He knew that crossing Ladinda would be professional suicide. He was tired of the way that she thought that she could play with people's lives. Calli was missing, and it was all Ladinda's fault. He had to find her.

Something ahead caught Sham's eye. At first he thought that his eyes were playing tricks on him, but he still decided to investigate. As the wind blew he realized that he did indeed see something. He rushed to a bush and saw that several strands of hair were caught in it. They were the same length and color as Calli's. She had been there! "CALLI!!!!!" he called louder than ever. She had to be close.

Chapter Twenty-Five

After calling Calli's name several times and not getting an answer, Sham decided that he needed to look for more clues. He searched for footprints, additional hair, and trampled brush. He didn't find anything out of the ordinary. "Think, Sham," he said out loud. "Gren's the smartest person that you know. What would she do? She'd try to wander, that's what she'd do. Maybe that's not a bad idea. If Calli is around here somewhere, she knows that we'll be trying to contact her."

Sham took the bag off of his back and sat down on a rock. He closed his eyes and reached out. He wasn't as good at wandering unknown areas as Gren and Lawson were. He could usually find Titus, but he wasn't sure what to look for with Calli.

The first dream that Sham found he instantly recognized as Titus'. He didn't want to talk to him, so he immediately left it. He hoped that he had been undetected. He decided to search for a dream in a different area. Wandering was not an exact science, and wandering distances made even less sense. A lot of it had to do with feelings and gut instincts. A natural born gift, talent, and ability were a big part of it as well, which was why Gren had such a promising future. She had more talent when it came to wandering than the rest of them put together.

Sham opened his eyes. "What would Calli dream about?" He took a deep breath and tried to reach out again. Soon he saw a dream and entered it. The dream was cloudy, but he was able to recognize Calli and Tayo walking down a road. They were talking and laughing.

"Calli?" Sham said into the dream. The dreamer would be able to hear his voice but wouldn't see him. It was against the rules in a clinical wandering session to refer to the client by name, but it didn't matter when wandering friends.

"Sham? ..... you?" It wasn't Calli's voice that answered, it was Tayo's.

Sham was disappointed. "Oh, sorry, I was looking for Calli."

"So, am ..... you think that you're doing? Do you know how dangerous .... out there on your own?"

"Do you know how dangerous it is for Calli to be out here on her own?" Sham's voice answered. "It's my fault that she's missing, so I'm going to find her."

"It's not ... fault," the dream-Tayo replied. Dream-Calli, who was still standing next to her friend, nodded in agreement.

"Tell that to Titus," Sham's voice said. "Listen, have you heard from Calli? Anything?"

"No, I ..... to make contact. Neither has Gren. Calli knows ..... trying to wander, Sham. I'm ..... worried."

"I'm going to find her," Sham's voice promised. "I think I'm getting closer."

"Really?" Both the dream-Tayo and the dream-Calli perked up.

"She's been where I am right now," Sham's voice explained. "I found some strands of hair. I tried calling her, but didn't get an answer. That was when I decided to try to wander."

"Where...?" the dream-Tayo asked.

Sham struggled to maintain contact. He had never had such a difficult time wandering before. "What was that? You're breaking up."

"Where are you?"

"So, you can tell Titus? Nice try, but I'm not saying. Keep dreaming, Tayo. I'll let you know when I find her." Sham exited the dream and opened his eyes. Knowing that no one had been able to contact Calli made him feel a lot worse.

· ○ ●◉● ○ ·

Tayo opened her eyes, stood up, and stretched. She was tired of dreaming. She knew that she needed to keep doing it, but it was getting difficult. There was a trick to communicating through wandering, and the dreamer needed to be able to keep the dream going. There was a fine line between a dream-like state and actually falling asleep and dreaming a real dream. Their craft was meant to help people through their subconscious minds, it wasn't really meant as a means of communicating.

Part of her felt a little bit better after talking to Sham. It had been a strange conversation, sometimes she had a hard time understanding what he said. She did realize that he had found a sign of Calli, but he hadn't been able to wander her either. Sham and Calli had a growing bond, and that should have made it easier for him to find her dreams. There had to be a reason that Calli wasn't reaching out or trying to dream herself. Tayo didn't like the possibilities of why no one had been able to make contact with her.

Tayo sat down and decided to try to wander. She'd reach out and look for Calli. If that didn't work, she would once again dream. The problem was that she was running out of things to dream about.

· ○ ●◉● ○ ·

Sham decided to dream for a little while himself. After all, if Calli wasn't dreaming, she would probably be trying to wander. Sham closed his eyes and allowed his mind to drift. Soon he saw himself walking along the beach with Calli. They were holding hands.

"Sham, I don't ...... trying to prove, but you're just ..... matters worse."

The dream changed. Calli was gone, and Sham was standing alone near where they kept the supplies. "Titus, stay out of my dream. I really don't feel like dealing with you right now."

"Fine, you don't ..... listen to me," Titus' voice said. "Hold on a micro. Just don't .... dreaming."

Sham considered ending the dream, but decided against it. He hadn't given Calli enough time to look for him.

"Sham, it's me," Gren's voice said. "Are .... okay?"

"Yeah, I'm fine. I'm just looking for Calli. And Gren, you're breaking up a bit. Titus was too."

"We .... to Tayo. She said that ..... some of Calli's hair," Gren's voice said. "Let ..... where you are, and ..... look from there."

The dream-Sham shook his head. "No, Gren, I'll find Calli on my own. I'm not heading back to camp until I find her."

"There's str .... bers." This time it was Lawson's voice.

"Did Titus come back as well?" the dream-Sham asked. "I feel like there's a party going on in my head."

"No," Gren's voice informed him. "He didn't want ..... invade your privacy."

"But you and Lawson have no problem doing that."

"It's ..... like that ..... know it." Gren's voice stayed calm, it was no wonder that she was considered a top wandering prospect.

Calli reappeared in Sham's dream. "I gotta go, guys," he said. "I've taken too much time out of my search as it is. And you're breaking up like crazy, it's hard to understand what you're trying to say. I'm gonna go find Calli now. Bye."

"Just ..... know where you..." Gren's voice started to say, but Sham stopped dreaming before she could finish.

· · ●◐○ · ·

"That was pointless," Sham said out loud. He hadn't learned any new information, and instead of finding Calli he had been lectured by some of his closest friends. Just a couple of rotations earlier he had thought that his life was close to perfect, but now everything seemed to be going wrong. His girl was missing, his best friend hated him, and his other friends thought that he was incompetent. He intended to prove them all wrong.

Sham decided to look again near where he had found the hair. Maybe he had missed something. "It was probably still dark when she came through here, so she'd look for the easiest footing." Sham made an educated guess and walked in the direction that seemed to make the most sense. After walking for ten hundreds he thought that maybe he had made a mistake, but then he found a much larger clue. There was a small creek with muddy footprints near it. Sham hoped that the footprints would lead him straight to Calli.

Chapter Twenty-Six

Sham wanted to run as he followed the footprints, but he knew that he needed to be careful. He was getting close, he was sure of it. He noticed that there was another set of footprints as well, they were barefoot. "She was following the person who took our food," Sham said out loud. "She probably saw him take the blanket. He better not have hurt her."

After a unit the creek went in one direction while the footprints went off in another. It didn't take long for them to fade. "CALLI!!!!!" Sham called for the hundredth time that rotation. There was still no answer.

Since there were no more footprints to follow Sham had to make another educated guess. "The food-thief probably knows this island well, so he'd have a way that he normally goes." Sham looked around and realized that the brush was not as thick in one area. It looked a bit trampled. "That way." Before leaving the creek he took out the analyzer. The water was safe for drinking, so he took a long drink from the bottle that he had with him and then filled it up again. He needed to make sure that he had enough water for Calli once he found her. There were some root vegetables growing near the creek, so Sham used the analyzer on those as well. He filled up his bag, and kept one out for himself. He took a bite. "Disgusting," he said. As bad as it was, the food gave him an energy burst, so he took another bite as he started forward. "I'm coming, Calli," he said.

· ○ ○◉○ ○ ·

"This is pointless," Titus said to his friends. They had just taken a break to wander. He had no idea why Ladinda had not made contact with him.

"What's really strange is that I wasn't able to find any dreams off of this island," Gren said. "I can find Tayo with some effort, but the further we've hiked from our camp, the harder it's been to find any other dreams."

"Still looking for tonic?" Lawson asked.

Gren glanced at Titus. They both knew that tonic wasn't being used at the Learning Center. "Yeah, but it's not just that. I haven't been able to find a trace of any dreams anywhere, except for Tayo, Angel, and Dod. And of course Sham, but I think he's now avoiding us."

"I wonder if there are some conditions where dreams can't be found," Titus said. He had never heard of that, but it would explain why Ladinda hadn't wandered his dreams lately.

"We'll have to ask Haas about that when we get home," Lawson said.

Gren laughed. "You know Haas. Everything has to be clinical with him. He'd look at us like we were crazy."

"You're right." Lawson paused. "We'll have to ask Hutch about it when we get home."

"Anyone but Ladinda," Titus said. There was a hint of anger in his voice.

"Why?" Lawson asked. "What did Ladinda do?"

Titus still didn't want to give Lawson any information. "She should have sent someone to find us by now."

"True." Lawson seemed to buy the explanation. "Let's get going. We've got a lot of ground to cover."

"Yeah, thanks to Sham," Titus mumbled.

Tayo decided to take a break from dreaming. It was getting harder for her. Angel and Dod had been taking turns getting into dream-like states themselves. Tayo thought that it wouldn't hurt anything to let one of them be the point of contact for half a unit or so. It was Dod's turn. The two Purples had made a lot of progress, they had learned more than they would have in the classes that they were missing at the Learning Center. Tayo sat down next to the fire circle. There was no fire burning, but it was better than staring at the water. When they first arrived Tayo thought that the scenery was beautiful, but she was starting to not care if she ever saw the ocean again.

Angel sat down next to Tayo. "Taking a break?" she asked.

Tayo nodded. "You wouldn't think that dreaming is hard work, but it can be."

"I know what you mean." Angel paused. "You're really worried about her, aren't you." It wasn't a question.

"She's my best friend. I don't know what I'd do without her." Tayo sighed. "We weren't always this close. In fact, when we first became partners at the Learning Center we hated each other. But then circumstances made us have to work together, and we've been inseparable ever since."

"Kind of like Dod and me. We've been forced to work together the past few rotations, and we're actually starting to trust and like each other."

Tayo thought for a micro. There were some similarities between their current situation and what had happened during her Green orbit. That had been a setup. Could Ladinda have done it to them again? "So, he's not so bad after all?"

Angel smiled. "He's actually a lot of fun. Back at the Learning

Center my friends all tease me about being partnered with a boy. I think that I let what they said go to my head, and I blamed him for something that was beyond our control."

"Don't listen to your friends, Angel. Your relationship with your partner is much more important than their opinions. If they're really your friends, they won't pick on you about something as important as who you're partnered with."

"I realize that now."

Sham decided to take a micro and try to wander again. He had finally realized that he was being selfish, and that looking for Calli alone was probably not the smartest idea. He decided to tell Tayo or Gren where he was. He knew that he was close. He reached out for any sign of Calli. He wasn't able to find her, but he did discover Angel and Dod making a sculpture in the sand. The dream was weak, Sham knew that he would have to concentrate in order to maintain contact. "Nice sand sculpture," his voice said.

"Thanks," the dream-Dod replied. "Angel and I ..... working on it for units. At least ..... like it's been that long."

Sham concentrated to stay in the dream. He had never had such a difficult time wandering before. "Listen, Kid," his voice said. "do me a favor and let Tayo know that I've been following some footprints. I think that I'm getting closer."

The dream-Dod put down the stick that he had been digging up sand with. "Tayo said that if you ..... that I'm supposed ..... out where you are."

"Tell her that I found the footprints near..."

The dream was gone.

"I didn't realize how close I was to getting kicked out of the program," Angel continued. "Gren pointed that out to me. When we get back, if my friends don't ease up a bit, I'm going to ask to change rooms. I'd rather have roommates who don't pick on me all the time."

"That's how Calli and I got to know Gren so well," Tayo informed the young Purple. "Ladinda had us move in with her when we were Greens, even though she's an orbit older than we are. There were two other Blues in the room as well."

"It must have been a big room."

"Sham found footprints." Neither Angel nor Tayo had realized that Dod was there. "He wanted me to tell you that he's been following them."

"Sham wandered you?" Tayo was excited. "Did he say anything else?"

"He just said that he thinks that he's close. It was weird, I think that he was having a hard time wandering. He was going to tell me where the footprints are, but then he was gone."

"Thanks, Dod," Tayo said. "You did well. I should probably try to contact Gren, let her know what's going on." Knowing that Sham had found another sign of Calli gave Tayo hope. She just couldn't understand why Calli wasn't dreaming.

Sham was confused after contacting Dod. He didn't know why it had been so difficult to maintain contact. Wandering had been easier back when he was a Red and he had his first practical classes. He didn't know how much information he had been able to pass on. He hoped that it would be enough, since he had finally realized that searching alone was not a good idea.

The broken branches and trampled down brush told Sham that he was probably headed in the right direction. Someone went that way often. Suddenly the path stopped. Sham had no idea where to go. "CALLI!!!!" he called again.

"Sham?" a voice weakly replied.

Chapter Twenty-Seven

"Calli!" It was the happiest micro of Sham's life. "Hold on, Kiddo, I'm coming!"

"Sham, be careful. The footing is..."

Before Calli could finish her warning, Sham took a step forward. The ground gave out underneath him. He tried to grab hold of something, anything, to break his fall, but it was no use. He braced himself as he fell, hoping to minimize any physical damage. The fall was equal to two stories, and somehow he landed on his feet.

"You did that a lot more gracefully than I did," Calli said.

"Calli!" Sham hurried over to her. There wasn't a lot of light, but he could see that she was sitting on the ground. When she didn't get up, he bent down and gave her a hug. "Are you okay? What's wrong?"

"When I fell through that same hole I landed on my ankle. I think it's broken. Otherwise, I'm fine."

"Are you hungry?" When Calli nodded Sham took the bag off of his back. He handed it to her. "I have both food and water."

"Thank you, Sham." Calli gratefully took the pack from him. She took a long drink and then took a bite of one of the vegetables. "This tastes a lot better than it did the last time that I ate."

"So, where are we? And how do we get out of here?"

"We're in a cavern or something. I haven't been able to explore because of my ankle, so I don't know if there's a way out or not. I know that there's water somewhere, I can hear it in the distance."

"I need to figure out how to get you out of here." Sham walked around the large area that they were in and couldn't find an exit, except for the one overhead. There was no obvious way to get to it.

"I was beginning to think that no one was going to come looking for me," Calli said.

"You're kidding, right? We've done nothing but look for you. Of course, you could have helped by dreaming or trying to wander. It would have been a lot easier if you let us know where you were."

"I've been both dreaming and wandering! Constantly! The only time I stopped was when I heard you call my name. I haven't found one dream, and no one has found mine."

Sham continued to look around. "That's strange, because we've been trying to find you. Earlier I was wandering Dod, and I had a hard time staying in his dream. I wonder if there's something on this part of the island that is blocking the dreams or something."

"Declan once told Tayo and me that sometimes atmospheric conditions can affect the ability to wander, especially with distances." Calli took another bite of the vegetable and washed it down with more water.

Sham looked confused. "Who is Declan?"

Calli shook her head. "The Wanderer that Tayo and I apprentice for."

"Oh yeah." Sham sat down next to Calli. His eyes had finally adjusted to the dim light. "Let me take a look at that ankle."

Calli shifted slightly and the pain was obvious across her face. "You don't have any medical experience."

"True, but I'm all you've got right now. Plus I can tell a broken bone when I see one." Calli's shoe and sock were already off. Her ankle was swollen to over twice its normal size, and it was badly bruised. "That's definitely broken."

"Thanks, Sham, you're so helpful."

Sham sat back and leaned against the cavern wall. "Don't worry, we'll be out of here soon."

"How do you know?"

"When I wandered Dod, I told him as much as I could about where I was looking. He'll pass that info onto Gren, Lawson, and What's-his-name, and they'll be here soon. Plus I'm not going to give up on finding a way out."

"'What's-his-name'? You mean Titus?" For the first time Calli noticed the cut on Sham's face. "Sham, what happened to your eye?"

"Titus looks worse." Sham paused. "He blamed me for your being gone, because I fell asleep. And he's right. I'm sorry I let you down, Calli."

"Sham, it wasn't your fault. It was just one of those things. I saw the blanket moving, so I took off and followed. I wasn't thinking, and I didn't even know that you were asleep."

"I was sure that the man who stole our food had grabbed you as well."

Calli shook her head. "He's not a man, he's a boy. He's probably close to Angel and Dod's age."

"A boy? He must have pretty big feet. Did you catch up to him?" Sham picked up the water and took a short sip. He didn't want to use all of their water but he also wanted to keep his strength up.

"No. I think I spooked him. He was way far ahead of me when I took a wrong step and ended up in here. He was so far ahead that I don't think that he knew that I fell."

"I wonder how someone that age ended up here on this forsaken island. Did you call after him or anything? Did he seem to understand what you were saying?"

"Yeah, I called out to him," Calli replied. "The only thing that he yelled back was, 'Don't hurt us!' His clothes were torn and too small, like he's grown a lot since he got them."

Sham thought for a micro. "He said 'us'? Are you sure?"

Calli nodded. "I thought it was strange too."

Sham stood up again. "Will you be okay alone for a few hundreds? I'd like to explore and see if there's another way out of here."

"I'll be fine."

"Okay, Kiddo. See you in a little bit."

"So, tell me exactly what he said." Gren, Lawson, and Titus were back on the beach with the others. Lawson was trying to find out anything that he could from Dod.

"He wanted me to tell Tayo that he had been following footprints, and that he was getting close. He was about to tell me that the footprints were near something, but then he was gone."

"He didn't give you any other clues as to where he could be?"

Dod shook his head. "I could tell that he was having a hard time staying in the dream."

"Thanks, Kid, good job. That's really helpful information."

Lawson joined Gren and Titus, who were standing not too far away. "All he knows is what Tayo already told us. He also said that it seemed like Sham was having a hard time staying in the dream."

"There's something strange going on with the dreams around

here," Titus commented. "At first we didn't have a problem, but now it's getting harder to find them."

Gren squinted as she thought for a micro. "The other night, the one when Calli went missing, the wind picked up for a little while. Something just felt different. I wonder if that's somehow connected to our wandering problems."

"That wouldn't explain why you haven't been able to get in touch with the Learning Center," Lawson pointed out. "You haven't been able to reach them the entire time that we've been here."

Gren and Titus exchanged knowing glances. Lawson didn't notice. "Well," Gren said in an attempt to change the subject, "we need to think logically if we're going to find where Sham is searching."

"If we're talking about Sham, logic has nothing to do with it," Titus quickly added.

Gren ignored the comment. "We know that he started over near the supplies. Most likely he headed off in the direction where we found the piece of torn cloth."

"Dod said he was following footprints," Lawson added. "Mud would make great footprints. Maybe he's near the creek that shoots out from that area that we found. You know the one, at the clearing where Angel and Dod had such a good time playing in the water." Lawson smiled at Gren. A lot more had happened there than just the two Purples playing in the water.

"We'll head that way and follow the creek," Gren said. "Sounds like a plan."

Gren, Lawson, and Titus filled Tayo in on where they were going to search. They promised that they would be gone for only a couple of units. They would then return, unless they were able to communicate by wandering. The three friends headed out once again to look for Calli and Sham.

· · ○●○ · ·

The cavern was huge. The only light was from holes in the ceiling. Sham wished that he had another light source, but there wasn't much that he could do about it. He decided to think logically and listen. Calli said that she had heard water in the distance, he wanted to find it. Maybe that would provide them with a way out.

The problem with the sound in the cavern was that it echoed. Several times Sham thought that he was headed in the right direction, only to find a dead end. When he saw the water source he was immediately disappointed. There was moving water but there was no space that was large enough for him to fit through, let alone get an injured Calli out. He checked the water with the analyzer, it was safe to drink.

"Calli!" he called loudly. "I need your voice to find my way back. This place is gigantic."

"I'm in here, Sham!" Calli called back. "Any luck?"

Making his way back to where Calli was seated was a lot easier than finding the water source. "Well, the good news is that the water is safe to drink. There's no food, though. I was hoping to find something growing along the side, but I guess that there's not enough light."

"I take it you didn't find a way out."

Sham shook his head. "We'll just have to wait for Gren and Lawson. There was a rope ladder back on the MAAD, we'll make Titus swim out to get it. We'll get out of this soon, Kiddo."

"Why do you keep calling me that?"

Sham took a few steps towards the direction that he hadn't yet explored. "Because if I call you 'Sweetheart' you'll probably slug me." Even in the dim light Calli could see Sham's smile.

"You've got that right." Calli waited until Sham was out of sight to smile herself. Even though their situation seemed hopeless, she was suddenly filled with hope.

Chapter Twenty-Eight

"I feel like I'm always traipsing through the woods, trying to find someone," Titus complained as he stepped over a small branch.

"It's not that bad," Lawson said.

"Sure it is. In our final orbit, we were looking for you and Gren. And then last orbit..." Titus let his words drop.

Gren finished his sentence for him. "It was Winnie. You don't have to act like it never happened. She and Mollie are doing quite well this orbit. No more problems."

"So, it worked?" Titus asked.

"Yeah. It seems to have." Gren grinned. "You're right, there do seem to be some similarities between this time and our final orbit at the Learning Center."

"Except we've never had the same problems wandering," Lawson added. "It's getting more difficult each time that we try."

"We're almost to the watering hole," Gren said. "Have you seen it yet, Titus?"

He shook his head no. "I always went the other way, towards where we found the food."

"It's gorgeous," Gren said. She glanced at Lawson. "It's a really special spot."

Titus remembered something that Lawson had told him. "Is it where..." Lawson shot Titus a quick glance, hoping that his friend was not going to mention the kiss that Gren had given to him. "Is it where Angel and Dod first started getting along?"

Gren didn't notice the glance. "Yeah. And the water is clean, we tested it before."

"I still brought the analyzer," Lawson said, holding it up.

"Good idea. It's up this way, Titus. Prepare to be amazed."

Titus had pictured in his mind what the spot would look like, but his imagination didn't compare to the real thing. "Wow. You're right, that's incredible."

"Too bad we don't have time to enjoy it," Lawson said. "We have to find our other roommate."

"Yeah, our dwelling is going to be a lot of fun once we get home," Titus said.

Sham kept going back and forth between exploring the cavern and sitting with Calli. He was sure that there had to be a way out, but the more he explored, the larger the cavern seemed. He didn't like to leave Calli for very long, and part of him was scared that he was going to get lost. The only light was still from overhead. He turned a corner and noticed something on the ground. He picked it up, and even in the dim light he could tell that it was some type of mechanical gear. Directly overhead there was a fair amount of light shining through a hole. He looked up, the hole was perfectly round, unlike the other holes in the ceiling that he had discovered. He decided to show the gear to Calli.

It took Sham a micro or two to get his bearing and figure out which way he needed to go. "Hey Kiddo, I need your voice," he called.

"I'm this way, Sham," she replied. Less than a hundred later he was back.

"Look what I found." He handed the gear to Calli.

Calli looked it over. "How did that get in here?"

"I don't know, but I doubt that we're the only two people who have been in this place. Which tells me that there's got to be a way out of here, I just need to find it."

Gren, Lawson, and Titus found the creek that ran off from the watering hole and started to follow it. They weren't sure if it was the same creek that Sham had followed, but it was the best chance that they had of finding him and hopefully Calli. They looked for other clues as well, such as broken branches and trampled down grass. Lawson was starting to feel like they were heading in the wrong direction when Gren pointed. "Look!" she said excitedly, "Footprints!"

Tayo, Angel, and Dod took turns dreaming so that someone would be able to contact them. They weren't having any luck. Tayo insisted that they all eat something to keep their strength up. The food was terrible, but they were hungry so they all munched on the root vegetables. After she had eaten it was Angel's turn to dream again. Out of curiosity, Tayo decided to wander Angel's dream. She could enter the dream but she was able to maintain contact for only a few micros. Whatever was making them not be able to wander was getting worse.

Gren, Lawson, and Titus all studied the footprints. They didn't want to make a mistake when they were getting close. There were three sets of footprints. "Those are Sham's," Titus said, pointing. "His feet are huge."

"I bet those are Calli's," Gren said, looking closely at the second set of footprints. "And these are barefoot. The man who stole our food?"

"If those are a man's footprints, he must be pretty small," Lawson commented. "They look more like they'd belong to Angel or Dod."

"So, a child stole our food?" Gren didn't try to hide the surprise in her voice.

"Why didn't we realize that the footprints belonged to a child when we first found them by the supplies?" Titus asked.

"Those weren't as clear as these are," Gren pointed out. "Mud preserves footprints better than sand does. I wonder how a child ended up on this island. Maybe he needs our help."

"At least there's no blood in them this time," Lawson said.

"Honestly, I think we need to first concentrate on finding Sham and Calli," Titus said. "After we find them, we'll see if we can help this kid."

"You're right." Gren stood up and looked off in the distance. Something caught her eye, a movement. "Stand still, both of you."

"Why?" Lawson asked.

"Because we're being watched. Straight ahead. I don't want to scare him."

Chapter Twenty-Nine

Gren slowly took a few steps forward. As she did, the young boy took off running. "Wait!" she called after him. "We're not going to hurt you, we just want to talk. We're looking for our friends!"

The boy ran faster, he obviously knew the area well. Gren ran after him. Lawson looked at Titus, and the two immediately followed.

"I didn't know that your girlfriend could run so fast," Titus said, trying to catch his breath.

"She's full of surprises," Lawson panted back.

"And I'm not his girlfriend," Gren said. She was ahead of them and wasn't breathing heavily. "At least not yet. Come on, we need to catch up to him."

∘ ∘ ⦿ ● ⦿ ∘ ∘

"I want to try an experiment," Calli said. "Come, sit down."

Sham sat down on the cavern floor next to Calli. He was once again holding the gear. "What can I do for you, Kiddo?"

"First, you can stop calling me that. Then again, it's better than the alternative, so forget I said anything. You said before that you were trying to wander me, right?"

"Yeah, we all were trying."

"Let me try to wander you. Right here and now. Something strange is going on, and if we can't wander when we're this close to each other, something is definitely wrong."

Sham smiled. "Are you sure that you're ready for what I might decide to dream about?"

Calli rolled her eyes. "Dream about your glidemobile."

"That's boring, compared to what I want to dream about, but I'll do it for you." Sham closed his eyes and let his mind drift into a dream-like state.

Calli couldn't sit in her normal wandering position because of her ankle, so she just tried to get as comfortable as possible. She reached out and attempted to touch Sham's dream. She couldn't find it.

After a hundred or so Sham opened his eyes. "Let me try to wander you. I've always wondered what you dream about."

Calli rolled her eyes again. "Okay, we'll try." They reversed the process. It still did not work.

· ·○●○· ·

The boy was faster than Gren and he knew the woods better than she did. She did her best to follow him but eventually he was out of sight. Lawson and Titus caught up a few micros later.

"So..." Titus said, trying to catch his breath, "what do we do now?"

"We, well, we look for more clues, I guess." Gren wasn't breathing hard. She was discouraged, for some reason she was sure that the boy would be able to lead them to Calli and Sham.

"Look!" Lawson said, pointing. He took a couple of deep breaths. "There he is...across the clearing!"

Gren headed directly towards where the boy was standing. Lawson and Titus were close behind her.

"No!" the boy screamed loudly. It was the first time that they heard him speak.

Sham sat close to Calli. "I'm sorry," he said.

"For what?" Calli asked.

"For two things. First, because I haven't done a very good job of rescuing you."

"That's not your fault," Calli said. "I never should have taken off like that. I was stupid, I shouldn't have followed the boy without telling anyone where I was going."

"Okay," Sham said with his trademark grin, "you can take the credit for that one. But there is something else that I'm sorry for."

"What?"

Sham looked away. "I've been putting pressure on you, trying to push you into a relationship that you might not be ready for."

"Sham..."

"It's just that, I don't know, I've liked you for a long time now, and I thought that maybe you felt the same way. It's like we have this connection, but, I don't know, maybe you don't feel it."

"Sham..."

"So, I'm not going to ask you to be my girl, as much as I want to. Instead, think about one date, once we get home. I'll take you out to dinner, to a restaurant of your choice, and we can hang out for a while, just you and me. And then, maybe, you'll see that we do have an 'it'."

"Sham!"

"What?"

"I'd love to go on a date with you. I think you're right, there could be something between us. I want to find out."

"Seriously?"

Calli leaned close to Sham. She jabbed her finger into his arm. "Poke."

"Hey, no fair! I thought that we had called a truce."

There was a loud noise in a different part of the cavern, accompanied by a scream. Sham sprang to his feet. "Stay here, I'm going to check that out."

"It's not like I can go anywhere," Calli said.

Sham was gone for less than a hundred. "Honey, set a few extra places at the table for dinner," he called. "We have company." He reentered the area where Calli was sitting. Standing behind him, covered with dirt and mud, were Gren, Lawson, and Titus.

Chapter Thirty

"They were lucky," Sham informed Calli. "When they broke through they didn't fall nearly as far as we did. It's still too high to get out, though."

Gren ran over to Calli and immediately saw that she was hurt. "Are you okay? Your ankle looks like it's broken."

"That's what I told her," Sham said.

"That hurts, but I'm fine otherwise," Calli said. "What are you guys doing here? What happened?"

"We came to rescue you," Titus said.

"Nice job," Sham remarked. "At least I thought to bring food and water."

Lawson looked down at his empty hands. He must have dropped the water bottle and the analyzer. "What is this place?"

"It's some type of underground cavern," Sham replied. "It's huge. There's fresh water, but I haven't found any food. We're also not the only people who have been in here." He picked up the single gear that he had found and handed it to Lawson.

"It looks like it came from a glidemobile."

"Yeah, that's what I thought. I figure that someone else was here at some point, so there has to be a way out. Since you guys decided to join us, it will be easier to look. I didn't want to leave Calli alone for too long."

"Why don't you show Lawson and Titus where you found it?" Calli suggested. "Gren will stay here with me."

Sham squatted down next to Calli. "It figures that they'd interrupt our conversation. Lousy timing."

Calli smiled. "I'm pretty happy with what we accomplished."

Sham winked at Calli. "I knew that I was irresistible."

"I wouldn't go that far."

"This will be a great story to tell our grandkids. How we first realized that we were meant to be while stuck in a cavern on some deserted island."

"Grandkids?" Calli repeated.

"Too soon?"

Calli nodded. "Let's make it through our dinner date first. And Sham, you were wrong. Titus doesn't look worse."

Tayo was not sure what she should do. Gren, Lawson, and Titus had been gone much longer than they had said that they would be. She had tried dreaming and tried wandering without any trace of any of them. She decided to give them a few more hundreds, and then she would go search for everyone herself.

"So, how did you end up down here?" Calli asked Gren.

"We were looking for the two of you. Sham had let Dod know about a set of footprints that he had been following, and we were able to find those. We then saw a young boy. I tried to catch up to him, but he outran me. We then saw him again. I started to walk towards him, and he screamed 'no'. That was when the ground gave out and all three of us fell."

"So, you saw him too?"

"Yeah. The poor kid looks like he's been stuck here for a long time."

"I think he's the one who took our food," Calli said. "I left out a blanket, and I saw him when he took it. I ran after him, and that's when the ground gave out on me and I ended up in here. Sham is blaming himself because he fell asleep, but I didn't even check to see if he was awake. I just ran after the kid."

"Did the boy say anything to you?" Gren asked.

"That's the weird part. He yelled 'Don't hurt us'."

"He said 'us'?"

Calli nodded. "I thought that it was kind of strange too. I don't think that he's here alone." She paused. "And then there's the whole wandering thing, that's been off as well."

"What do you mean?"

"Sham said that you guys have all been trying to wander me. I have been both dreaming and trying to wander ever since I fell, but no contact was made. I couldn't find anything! And then Sham and I tried an experiment. We sat as close as you and I are to each other and tried to wander. We couldn't. I don't know if there was a shift in the atmosphere or it's the stone walls of this cavern or what, but you have to admit that something unusual is going on."

Gren breathed a sigh of relief. "You don't know how happy I am to hear you say that."

"Gren, not being able to wander is not a good thing in a situation like this, or in our chosen profession."

"I know," Gren quickly replied. "But deep down I was scared that I was losing the gift. I'm so close to the Trials, and, well, it's nice to know that I'm not the only one who has been having a problem. I mean, Lawson and Titus both have said that something is off as well, but Lawson would say anything to make me feel better and I can't really believe anything that Titus says right now."

"Why not?"

Gren knew that she shouldn't let anyone else know about Ladinda's plan. It was also pretty obvious that Sham hadn't shared the details with Calli. "He and Sham have just been at it too much lately. They've both been thinking more with their anger than logically. I've never seen them this mad at each other before."

"They're mad because of me, aren't they?"

Gren shook her head. "They might be using your disappearance as an excuse, but I don't think that's the real problem. I think it's more the situation than anything. The Learning Center should have sent someone to find us by now. They're frustrated. Who am I kidding, I'm frustrated as well. It would be nice if we could make it through an entire orbit without getting into an impossible situation and have someone end up missing."

"I know what you mean." Calli grinned. "This has become our new normal."

∘ ∘ ◦ ● ◦ ∘ ∘

"This is where I found the gear," Sham said to Lawson. He pretended that Titus wasn't there. "Look up. That hole doesn't look like any of the others."

Lawson did as instructed. "It's perfectly round, like it was carved out on purpose."

"That's what I thought as well."

Titus waited a micro, then looked at the hole. "If that's how the gear got in here, it doesn't mean that there's a way out. It could have fallen in."

Sham rolled his eyes. "But who would drill a hole just to drop a gear down it? There's got to be more to it than that. Plus that's pretty high. There's no mark on the floor where I found the gear to indicate that something heavy had hit it from that distance. My guess is that the hole was drilled to provide light to whoever else has been in here."

"We're not alone on this island," Lawson said. "We were following a young boy, or rather we were trying to keep up with Gren, who was following a young boy. I think that he tried to warn us about this cavern, because he screamed 'no' right before we fell in."

"He's not alone," Sham said. "This is what happened with Calli, how she ended up here. She saw him steal the blanket, so she took off after him." Sham looked at Titus. "She didn't try to get me, she didn't even realize that I had fallen asleep. She just took off on her own." He turned his attention back towards Lawson. "Anyway, the only thing that the kid said to her was 'Don't hurt us'."

"Us?" Titus repeated.

"It's a word that is used to imply that there is more than one person. It's the plural form of the word 'me'."

"I know what the word means."

"So, the kid is not alone," Lawson commented. "Interesting."

* * * ● ● ● ○ ● * *

Tayo decided that she had waited long enough. She knew that the other three had headed towards the watering hole, but she wasn't really sure where that was. Everyone else had been able to go out and explore, but she always seemed to get stuck at the camp, watching the Purples and trying to wander. Angel and Dod knew where the watering hole was, so she asked them how to get there.

"Do you want us to come along?" Angel asked.

"No," Tayo said. "Someone should be here when the other three get back. I won't be gone long, I just feel like I should see if I can find them. I'm sure that they'll return. If they get back before I do, send Gren and Lawson to get me, okay?"

Angel and Dod weren't thrilled to be left behind once again, but they understood. Tayo grabbed some food and a bottle of water, and then left the camp.

Chapter Thirty-One

After showing Lawson and Titus where he had found the gear, Sham took them to the underground creek. They only had the water bottle that Sham had brought; the water and the analyzer that Lawson had been carrying had not made it with them when they fell. They filled up Sham's bottle and then went back and sat down with Calli and Gren to figure out their next step.

"So," Sham started, "we have plenty of water, but only one bottle to keep it in. We have a limited amount of food. Calli is hurt. We can't wander for some reason, and Tayo and the kids have no analyzer and no idea where we are. Do I have that right?"

"Tayo knows about the footprints," Gren said.

"Oh, so she'll come looking for us and end up in here as well," Sham said. "I feel so much better."

"I agree with what you said before, Sham," Lawson said. "I think that there's a way out, we just haven't found it yet. We need to keep looking."

Sham looked at Titus. "Anything new from Ladinda?"

"Ladinda?" Calli repeated.

"What does she have to do with anything?" Lawson added.

Sham stared hard at his former partner. "Ask Titus."

Titus wasn't sure if he should be upset or relieved. "We haven't been in contact again, Sham. Not since the time that you caught me."

"So, should we just assume that she's sending someone?" Sham asked. "Since she knows where we are."

"What are you two talking about?" Lawson was getting upset.

Titus decided that it was time to come clean. He knew that he didn't have any other choice, and deep down he believed that his friends all had a right to know the truth. "This whole trip was setup by Ladinda. The faulty fuel cell, drifting to the island, all of it. She did it so that Angel and Dod would have to trust each other, and look, it's worked."

"So, Ladinda really knows where we are?" Lawson asked.

Titus nodded. "She told me her plan back at the Learning Center, the rotation when she gave me the book for Cassidy. She instructed me to not tell anyone."

Lawson shook his head. "And we always do what Ladinda says. But wait, you told Sham."

"He caught me while Ladinda was wandering me. He knew I was being wandered and could tell that something was going on. So, I told him, and swore him to secrecy. But then he told Gren when Calli went missing, and that's been a big part of what we've been fighting about."

Lawson looked at Gren with pain on his face. "You knew that this was a setup and you didn't tell me?"

Gren wasn't sure how to reply. "Lawson...I..."

"I know. Ladinda has a reason for everything that she does. The difference, Gren, is that I would have told you."

"Has Ladinda said anything else?" Calli asked. She seemed to be the only one who wasn't getting emotional. "Like when she's sending someone to rescue us?"

"She hasn't wandered me again," Titus said. "Not since the time that Sham caught me. We have set times when I'm supposed to try to dream and there's been nothing."

"Ladinda is the best Dream Wanderer on Terra," Calli said. "If she can't wander you, there's definitely something strange going on."

"Why don't you try again," Gren suggested. "It won't hurt anything. Ladinda needs to know what's happening."

"That's a good idea." Titus stood up and took a few steps away. "It's easier for me to do this if no one is watching."

Lawson also stood up. He was still obviously upset. "I'm going to explore, see if I can find a way out."

Gren sprang to her feet. "I'm going with you." It wasn't a request.

Once they were alone Sham moved so that he was sitting close to Calli. "You're not upset with me, are you? I mean, I thought about telling you what I knew, but I didn't want to get your hopes up."

"I'm not upset," Calli replied. "Telling me wouldn't have helped the situation any."

"Good." Sham took Calli's hand. "I'd hate to think that I messed things up before our 'it' even got started."

"Just promise me one thing."

"Anything."

"Promise me that we'll never get like Gren and Lawson." Calli rested her head on Sham's shoulder.

"That's a promise, Kiddo." He thought about poking her, but decided instead that he'd rather have her head resting on him.

Tayo had no idea where she was. She thought that she had followed the directions that Angel and Dod had given to her, but hadn't found the watering hole. The footing was not easy, it didn't seem like anyone else had ever been that way. She had tried several times to wander, but couldn't find any dreams. She decided that it was probably a good idea to return to the camp on the beach. She turned around and realized in horror that she had no idea which direction she had come from.

· · ●●○ · ·

Lawson walked for a hundred without saying anything. Even though he was trying to stay ahead of her, Gren was right behind him. "Come on, Lawson. We need to talk about this."

After taking a few more steps, Lawson stopped and turned around. "You lied to me. You told me that they were fighting because Titus said that it was Sham's fault that Calli disappeared."

"I didn't lie," Gren explained. "That's exactly what started the fight. I've never seen Sham so mad. I just left out the part where Sham told me that Ladinda and Titus were working together."

"I can't believe that you didn't tell me. No, wait, I can believe it. That's the problem."

"Titus said that Ladinda didn't want anyone else to know." Even to Gren it sounded like a pretty lame excuse.

"That wouldn't have mattered to me if the situation were reversed. I would have told you."

"I know you would have. But Lawson, I'm not you. You know me better than anyone. Does it really surprise you that I didn't tell you? Or are you trying to change who I am?"

Lawson took a deep breath and let it out slowly. "You and your rules."

"Exactly! There are certain people who I don't want to cross, and Ladinda is at the top of that list. I haven't always agreed with her methods, but she has our best interests at heart. If she didn't want everyone to know what was going on I assumed that she had her reasons."

"But this whole situation has gone far beyond Ladinda and her plan."

"As far as we know." Gren lowered her voice. "Lawson, doesn't something feel a bit off here? Who says that this hasn't all been manipulated by Ladinda?"

"And Titus doesn't know?"

"That's what I'm thinking."

Lawson thought for a micro. "That would make sense. It's not like Ladinda hasn't gone to great lengths in the past."

"There's something big going on this time," Gren said. "Titus told me that they stopped using sleep tonic back at the Learning Center, that's why I wasn't able to pick up any traces. If Ladinda is going to change everything to help two Purples, I'm not going to get in her way."

Lawson nodded. "Okay, I understand why you didn't tell me. I'm not upset anymore. But I still would have told you."

Gren smiled at Lawson. "I already broke one rule for you on this trip. I'd pick breaking Haas' rule over telling you about Ladinda."

Lawson put his arm around Gren. "Me too. Want to break that rule again?"

Gren smiled. She was relieved that Lawson was no longer upset with her. "After the Trials. Maybe."

Angel and Dod sat as close as they could to each other without actually touching. "Dod, I'm scared. It looks like Tayo isn't coming back, and who knows what has happened to everyone else." Dod instinctively lifted up his arm to put it around his partner. All that he wanted to do was to comfort her. Angel immediately moved away. "No, Dod, we can't. Physical contact with a student of the opposite gender is against the rules."

"I'm sorry," Dod said. "I guess that I thought that it would be okay because no one else would know."

"We would know, Dod," Angel said. "That's what is important. Gren and Lawson were able to make it all the way through the Learning Center without breaking that rule. I want to be able to do the same thing. We can be the second set of male/female partners to make it all the way through the program."

"You want to still be my partner?" Dod asked.

Angel nodded. "The past couple of rotations you've been a better friend to me than any of the girls back at the Learning Center. I'm sorry that it took all of this for me to realize that."

"That's okay. I haven't been the best partner either."

"So, what are we going to do now?"

"I guess that we just wait. Maybe Tayo found them, and that's why it's taking her so long to come back. We need to believe that things are finally going to turn around and that we'll be back home soon." Dod hoped that Angel believed him because his words sounded hollow to him. If he couldn't comfort her physically, at least he could do his best to assure her with his words that everything would be fine.

There was a noise behind them that caused both Purples to jump. They turned around quickly. "Tayo?" Angel called out.

It was not Tayo who stood there.

Chapter Thirty-Two

The micro that Dod saw the stranger standing near them, he jumped to his feet and stood in front of Angel. He grabbed a piece of wood to use as a weapon if needed. The person standing there didn't look dangerous, but Dod wasn't going to take any chances. A boy who seemed to be about their age stood before them. His clothes were torn and were too small. He was barefoot.

When Angel saw the boy, she gasped. She was more confused than frightened.

"Please," the boy said to Dod, holding up his hands, "don't hurt me."

Dod thought for a micro, then put the wood down. He knew that they weren't in any danger. "Who are you? Where did you come from?"

"My name is Eli," the boy started. "My dad and I were out on the water a couple of orbits ago, and we got caught in a terrible storm. Our water craft was destroyed and I've been stuck here ever since. I'm sorry, I know I shouldn't have taken your food, but I couldn't resist. I hadn't had anything to eat but the stuff that grows on this island for so long. I just wanted to eat something that tastes good."

Angel got up and stood next to her partner. "We understand. I'm Angel, and this is my best friend, Dod. We're students at the Dream Wandering Learning Center."

"Oh, so that's what you've been doing," Eli said. "I've seen everyone sit down and zone out with their eyes closed. I've heard of dream wandering but I've never seen anyone do it before." He paused for a micro. "I was supposed to be a student at the

Mechanical Academy, but I never got the chance to start. When you first arrived here I thought that you were smugglers. But then I realized that none of you are cut out for that."

"Smugglers?" Angel repeated.

Eli nodded. "That's what I call them. They come by every couple of lunar cycles. They'll show up with some glidemobiles or something similar, then take them apart. I think that they're stolen and they sell the parts. The first time that I saw them I thought that maybe I was rescued, but then I realized that they would probably just kill me instead. They're not nice people. It's been a while since the last time that they were here, which was why I first assumed that was who you were, even though they hardly ever come to this side of the island. Then I saw everyone sit down and close their eyes, and I realized that you obviously weren't the smugglers."

"After you took the food," Dod said, "we saw that there was blood in the footprints. Was that yours?"

Eli nodded. "I outgrew my shoes a long time ago, so I just run around barefoot. It was dark, and I stepped on something. It wasn't a big deal."

"Have you seen anyone else?" Angel asked. "We were here with six other people, and they seem to keep disappearing."

"That's why I decided to say something to you," Eli explained. "Your friends need help."

After Titus informed everyone that he had not been contacted by Ladinda, they decided to keep exploring. Gren agreed to stay with Calli, while the other three searched for a way out. Sham was still sitting next to Calli as the decision was made. "Sham," Calli said softly before he got up, "I want you to do me a favor."

"Anything," he said.

"I want you to apologize to Titus."

Sham rolled his eyes. "Anything but apologize to Titus. He started it! Did I tell you what he said to me?"

Calli nodded. "Yes, but none of that matters. What matters is that the two of you are throwing away a friendship that you've had for orbits, all because of something that I did. Work it out with him. We all need each other if we're going to make it out of this mess. Remember, once we get out of this cavern we still have to find a way home. We need to work together as a team, like we have in the past." Calli looked directly into Sham's eyes. "Please do it for me."

Sham grinned. "Oh, so we're going to have that kind of relationship."

Calli smiled back. "If it works."

"Something else to tell the grandkids. 'All that Gram has to do is to look at me and blink a few times and I'll do whatever she wants. It even worked way back when we were stuck in that cavern...'"

"Sham, I agreed to one date."

"True, but you're not the only one who can use charm to get what you want." Sham winked at Calli and stood up. "You'll see, Kiddo."

As Tayo walked she realized that nothing looked familiar. She still hadn't found the watering hole, and she was pretty sure that she was not headed in the right direction to make it back to the camp. She wished that she had never decided to leave the two Purples behind, and hoped that they were okay.

• ◦ ○◉○ ◦ •

Sham, Lawson, and Titus decided to start looking again in the area where Sham had found the gear. There had to be a reason that a glidemobile gear had been sitting in the middle of nowhere. There wasn't much light, so Lawson felt along the stone wall to see if there was anything unusual. As he searched, Sham approached Titus. "Look, um, Titus, can we just forget everything that's been going on? Try to be civil to each other again?"

"I'm supposed to forget that you slugged me?"

"Oh come on. It's not the first time that I've slugged you, and it probably won't be the last. And this time you got me back."

"That's true."

"So, what do you say? I'd hate to think an orbits-long friendship is over just because you were a jerk to me."

"I was a jerk to you?"

"See, you admit it." Sham held out his hand. "How about it? Friends again?"

Titus ignored Sham's hand. "Didn't Calli tell you to apologize? Because I didn't hear anything that sounded like you're sorry in what you just said."

"I'm not the one who lied to everyone and conspired with Ladinda behind my friends' backs."

"Sham, I thought that you understood. This is Ladinda that we're talking about. The most powerful Dream Wanderer on Terra, and probably in the universe. If she had asked me to stand on my head and juggle I would have done it."

"Too bad she didn't," Sham replied. "That would have been a lot better than putting all of your friends in danger."

"Hey guys," Lawson called.

"Don't forget," Sham continued, "there's something weird

going on here with wandering. What if none of us can wander anymore? Maybe we've all lost the gift. If that's what has happened, all of our futures are at risk."

"Guys..."

"So, now it's my fault that we're having a problem with wandering?" Titus replied. "How did you jump to that conclusion?"

"Guys!" Lawson screamed. "Shut up for a micro and come here. I might have found something."

Gren sat down next to Calli. They could hear Sham and Titus fighting in the distance, but couldn't make out the words. "I asked Sham to apologize to Titus," Calli told her friend. "Obviously it's going well."

"So, what's going on between you and Sham?" Gren asked. "I mean, I know that you guys have had a mild flirtation going on for a while now, but it looks like it's become more than that."

"We're having grandkids."

"What?"

Calli laughed. "We're going to go out to dinner," she explained. "Once we get home, obviously. That's all I agreed to, one date, but Sham keeps talking about our grandkids."

"Would you expect anything else from Sham?"

Calli shook her head. "No. And it meant a lot to me that he came looking for me. Maybe he didn't go about it in the right way, he shouldn't have taken off alone, but then again I shouldn't have either. I can't tell you, Gren, how happy I was when I heard his voice. I was sure that no one would ever find me and that I was going to die down here. Of course, that's still a possibility if we can't find a way out."

"Even if we don't, Ladinda knows that we're on this island," Gren reminded her friend. "She's got to send a water craft eventually. Tayo has a general idea of which way we were headed, and then they'll find us. With a long enough rope ladder we'll all get out, even with your broken ankle."

Calli sighed. "I just hope that Tayo stays put. She has no sense of direction. If she decides to go out and look for us by herself, she's going to get lost."

"I doubt she'll leave camp. She knows what is at stake." Gren decided to try to lighten up the mood a bit. "I have some news. Lawson and I are in a pretty good place right now. We finally talked about all the things that I had been avoiding talking about. We're going to have a future together, even if it means that we can't both work for Haas."

Calli smiled. "It's about time. Gren, I was beginning to think that you would avoid that conversation forever."

"It was more than just a conversation." She lowered her voice to a whisper. "I kissed him."

Calli gasped. She had not expected to hear those words. "What about Haas? Wouldn't that be against his rules?"

Gren nodded. "Yup. But you know what? I don't even feel guilty about it. Calli, it was building up forever. I'm glad that I did it, and I don't even care that I broke a rule. Well, I don't care too much."

Calli laughed. "It's about time," she repeated.

Gren held up a hand. "You hear that?" Both girls were quiet for a micro. "Silence. Sham and Titus have stopped fighting."

"Or they've killed each other."

"Lawson would have stopped them." Gren paused. "I hope."

Sham and Titus stopped fighting and turned towards Lawson. "What did you find?" Sham asked.

"Come, feel here along the cavern wall." Lawson placed his hand on the stone and Sham and Titus did the same. "Feel that? Air is moving through that crack."

"So?" Titus asked.

"So, that means that there's something on the other side," Lawson explained. "Follow the crack with your hand. It goes all the way around."

"Which means that this rock isn't really part of the wall," Sham said.

Lawson nodded. "That's what I'm thinking. Maybe if we all push, we can get it to move." He stared at Sham and then Titus. "But it means that we'll have to work together, as a team."

"I'm willing if he is," Titus said quickly.

"I was the one who tried to apologize!" Sham reminded him.

"That wasn't much of an apology. You blamed me for everything!"

"Because it's all your fault!"

"Guys!" Lawson yelled again. "Work together as a team, remember?"

Sham, Titus, and Lawson all put their hands on the rock and pushed with everything that they had in them.

The further Tayo walked, the more lost she became. She didn't recognize anything. She tried to think logically, but it wasn't working. She tried wandering and found nothing. She also knew that she only had a couple more units until the sun would go down, and then she would be lost in the dark.

Tayo heard a stick break behind her. She turned around quickly but didn't see anyone. "Lawson?" she called out. "Gren? Titus? Is that you?" She saw a slight movement, someone was behind a tree. Tayo was pretty sure that it wasn't one of her friends.

Chapter Thirty-Three

Lawson, Sham, and Titus pushed with everything that they had in them, but the rock would not budge. They tried several times without any success. "There's got to be a way to move it," Sham said. "We need to keep trying. Our way out is on the other side."

"We don't know that," Titus corrected. "For all we know, there's just another room of the cavern on the other side. Plus we have no proof that this rock really does move."

"Way to try to kill my optimism, Buddy," Sham said. "But guess what, it didn't work. I still think that we're about to get out of here."

"Let's try again," Lawson suggested. "Maybe if we run into it and hit it with our shoulders?"

"I'm willing to try if he is," Titus said.

Sham rubbed his shoulder in anticipation, and then nodded. He knew that it was going to hurt, but it would be worth it to save Calli.

The group walked together to the far stone wall. They counted to three, then took off running towards the large rock.

"Over this way," Eli said. He led the two Purples to an open area. "Watch your footing, it's tricky. There's a cavern under here and there are openings all over the place. I tried to warn your friends when they were following me, but they kept going and all fell in. That was when I decided that I needed to make myself known to you two. If your friends are hurt, I can't get them out by myself."

"Where are we going?" Angel asked.

"You'll see in a hundred." Eli led them around the clearing, he didn't go straight across. "Some of the openings in the cavern ceiling are natural, and others were drilled by the smugglers so that there would be more light and fresher air down there. I don't know why they wanted to hide in a cavern or who they thought was going to try to find them. This island is deserted." Eli stopped and pointed at a large rock. "Here."

Angel and Dod looked at the rock and then at each other. "How are we going to move that?" Dod asked.

Eli smiled. "It's simple mechanics." He moved a couple of bushes and then pushed on a small rock that was on the ground. The large rock moved, revealing an opening. "The smugglers made sure that nothing looks out of the ordinary, but they have a hidden solar panel so that they have some power when they're here. They also use a generator inside, but they take that with them. I know this cavern well, so I'll go first." Eli bent and went through the opening. Angel and Dod followed close behind.

Once inside, the ground started to slope down sharply. "I think that this is the worst part for the smugglers," Eli commented. "They lower the glidemobiles down through a hole that they made, but they can't get them back out that way. Even with special dollies they sometimes have a hard time. Their language is terrible!"

"You seem to have spent a lot of time watching the smugglers," Dod pointed out.

Eli nodded. "There's not much else for me to do here. I always keep my distance, they have no idea that anyone lives on this island."

Angel blinked several times to adjust her eyes to the dim light.

"So, how do we get to our friends?" she asked.

"Right up ahead." Eli pointed at what appeared to be a solid stone wall. He felt along the side and pushed something.

"One more time, guys," Sham said. His shoulder was aching, but he didn't want to stop trying. "Let's do it for Calli and Gren."

The three of them walked back as far as they could, and then ran with all their might towards the rock. Right before they hit it, the rock moved out of its place. All three of them flew through the new opening and landed on the ground.

"Angel, Dod!" Lawson exclaimed. He got up and brushed himself off. "Am I ever glad to see you!"

Sham looked at Eli. "Who's your friend?"

"This is Eli," Dod explained. "His water craft crashed, and he's been stuck here for orbits." He looked at Eli, and then pointed. "That's Sham, Lawson, and Titus."

"Where is everyone else?" Angel asked.

"This way." Sham led the group back inside the other area. The rock started to slide closed behind them. "No, wait!" he screamed as he started back towards it.

"Don't worry," Eli said. He felt along the side and pushed something in the wall. The rock moved again. "I know how to get us out of here."

"At least the fighting has stopped," Calli commented.

"Yeah, but it would be nice to know what's going on," Gren added. "Do you think that they found something?"

Calli laughed. "Those three? Gren, you know very well that

they're going to need help to find us a way out of here."

"Did I hear something about finding a way out?" Sham was in the front, everyone else walked in behind him.

Angel took one look at Gren and ran towards her. "Gren!" she screamed. The two embraced. "Are you okay?"

"Yeah, we're all fine," Gren replied. "Except for Calli, her ankle is broken."

"But I'm okay otherwise." Calli looked and saw Eli standing behind Dod. "You! You're the one who took the blanket."

"I'm sorry about that," Eli said. "I didn't know that you were down here. I thought that you had stopped chasing me and returned to your camp. If I had known that you were hurt, I would have helped sooner."

Calli smiled. "That's okay."

Eli turned his attention towards Gren. "And I tried to warn you, when I realized that you were about to cross the clearing. Don't ever cross there, it's too dangerous."

"I realize that now."

Angel walked over and stood next to Eli. "This is our new friend Eli. He's stranded here as well. Eli, these are our other friends Gren, Calli, and..." Angel looked around. "Wait a micro, where is Tayo?"

"Tayo?" Gren repeated. "Isn't she with you?"

Angel shook her head. "She went looking for you units ago."

Sham shook his head. "Holy splarsh," he muttered to himself, "we lost another one."

Chapter Thirty-Four

Everyone realized that the most important thing was to get Calli out of the cavern. She had been in there the longest, and aside from minor cuts and bruises, she was the only one who was injured. Sham carried her in his arms, with her arms around his neck, through most of the cavern. "Give you any ideas?" he teased.

"Remember, it's not too late for me to change my mind about the one and only date that I agreed to."

"Point taken." He shifted Calli's weight slightly. "I'll behave."

Once they arrived at the slope that led outside the cavern they all realized that they had a problem. It was steep, and Sham knew that it would not be easy to continue to hold Calli the way that he had been carrying her.

"Sham, put me down, but not all the way," Calli said. "I have an idea." Sham put Calli down so that her good foot was on the ground. She kept her balance by holding onto him. "Titus, come here a micro." Titus took a few steps over and stood on the other side of Calli. She put one arm around him and kept the other one around Sham. She held her broken foot up. She was in a lot of pain, but she wasn't going to let that stop her. "Now, see, I need to rely on both of you to work together to get me out of here. Let's get to it, I don't ever want to see this place again."

"Maybe I should go first," Eli suggested. "I've been up and down here a hundred times, I can point out the places where the footing is rough."

"Good idea," Lawson agreed. "Eli, you take the lead, followed by Calli and those two, then Angel, Dod, Gren, and I'll go last. Everyone agree?"

When there were no objections, the group slowly started up the slope to finally leave the cavern. The rock at the top was still out of the way. Once everyone was outside, Eli hit the switch to make it close again. "Gotta make everything look normal in case the smugglers return," he said.

Sham and Titus helped Calli over to a rock so that she could rest for a micro. Even with help, the climb up the slope had taken a lot out of her. "So, what's next?" she asked.

"How about we breakup into two groups again?" Titus suggested. "Sham and the kids can get Calli back to our camp, and Gren, Lawson, and I will look for Tayo."

"No," Calli said quickly. "No more breaking up into groups. We need to stay together so that we don't run into trouble again."

"Tayo said that she would eventually head back to the camp," Dod pointed out.

"Yeah, she's probably back there now," Angel added, "wondering where Dod and I are."

"I can get you back there easily," Eli said. "I know the shortest way."

"Well, let's get going," Lawson said. "Are you up for it, Calli?"

Calli nodded. "I just want to see Tayo."

"So, how are we going to do this?" Titus asked. "Calli obviously still can't walk."

"I've got her," Sham said. He turned towards Calli. "We can travel faster if I carry you on my back. Will you be okay with that?"

"Yeah, I think so. But if I get too heavy, you'll let someone else take over, right?"

Sham got into a position so that Calli could easily put her arms around his neck and climb onto his back. "Sure, Kiddo. But I'll be fine."

Once he had picked her up Calli whispered into Sham's ear, "You know that you don't have to do this to impress me. I was impressed a long time ago."

"I'm not trying to impress you," Sham replied. "For once. I just want to get you back to camp. If I get tired, I'll let Lawson take over for a little while. I promise."

"What about Titus?" Calli asked.

"Who? I'm not sure who you're talking about."

Calli rolled her eyes. "Just so you know, I'm in the perfect position to poke you right now, and there would be nothing that you could do about it."

"Except drop you."

Calli slightly tightened her grip around his neck. "That's exactly why I haven't done it."

Gren walked close to Angel and Dod. Eli was a little bit ahead of them, he obviously knew the path well. "It's not too far, Gren," Angel said. "It didn't take long when Eli led Dod and me to find all of you."

"That must have been quite a surprise when he showed up at the camp," Gren commented.

"It was!" Angel exclaimed. "Dod was so brave. He stood in front of me to protect me...even though I didn't really need protecting."

"So, why did you decide to go with Eli?"

"Sometimes you need to trust someone," Dod replied. "We didn't know what else to do, and he knew where you were."

"I wonder how long he's been here," Gren said.

"He thinks it's been a couple of orbits," Angel answered.

"Well, as soon as our water craft gets here we can get him home as well," Gren said. "I bet there will be some people who are happy to see him alive!"

"Gren," Angel started, "how do we know that a water craft is coming for us? No one has been able to contact the Learning Center."

Gren realized that it was important that the two Purples did not find out that the entire trip was a trial that had been arranged specifically for them. "Because of what we've been saying all along. All that they have to do is to look at a map and they'll know where to search."

Eli, who was several steps ahead of them, turned around. "Did you say that they'll find this island on a map?" he asked.

Gren nodded. "That's how they'll know where to look for us. They have a general idea of where we were headed, and they can check the map and narrow it down from there. Once they send someone, Eli, you'll come with us. You'll finally get to go home!"

Eli turned back around so that the others couldn't see the worried look on his face.

No one was sure what to expect at the camp. They didn't know whether or not Tayo would be there. It was starting to get dark and they knew that searching for her at night might not be the best idea. They also did not want to leave her out by herself all night long if she was lost.

As they neared the camp Gren was the first one to notice something. She smelled smoke. As she exited the woods with the kids and walked toward the clearing she could see a fire burning.

"Gren!" Tayo screamed. She got up and ran towards the group.

"We found Calli," Gren said immediately. "Or rather, Sham found Calli, we found Sham, and then the kids found us. Calli's ankle is broken, but otherwise she's fine. They should be along in a micro, Sham is carrying her. Now give me a hug!"

Tayo hugged Gren, Angel, and then Dod. A micro later Titus and Lawson appeared, and she hugged them as well. "Sham and Calli are coming," Lawson informed Tayo. "He doesn't want to admit that he's getting tired."

Angel looked at Eli, and then at Tayo. "Hey Tayo, I want you to meet our new friend..."

"You're Eli, right?"

Eli nodded. "How did you know?"

At that micro a tired-looking Sham joined the group. Calli was still on his back. "Calli, you're okay!" Tayo screamed.

"Yeah, I'll be fine, thanks to Sham. Who can put me down any micro now."

Sham gently helped Calli get down to the ground. "See, I told you that I could do it."

"Excuse me," Eli said, "but you still didn't tell me how you knew my name."

"Oh, simple," Tayo replied. "Ryker told me." Everyone looked towards the fire. For the first time they noticed that there was a man sitting near it.

Chapter Thirty-Five

"Come on, everyone, we made some stew," Tayo said. "It's still not as good as what we're used to, but Ryker knew of a few plants that would help somewhat with the taste."

Titus looked confused. "Who is Ryker?"

"My dad," Eli replied.

"He saved me," Tayo added. "I was really lost, and he found me and brought me back here. Come on, I'll introduce you."

Sham picked up Calli again and carried her over near the fire. Everyone else walked there as well. They all sat down. The group from the cavern looked slightly confused. They had forgotten that Eli had used the word "us" and had assumed that Eli was living on the island alone.

Tayo passed out plates of food. "Ryker, these are my friends Calli, Sham, Lawson, Gren, Titus, Angel, and Dod."

"Nice to meet all of you," Ryker said. He looked to be at least 15 orbits older than any of them. "Although I wish that it could be under better circumstances."

"See, Dad, I told you that the smugglers weren't back."

"What is all of this talk about smugglers?" Sham asked. "Eli has mentioned them several times."

"They show up every couple of lunar cycles," Ryker explained. "They will usually have several expensive glidemobiles or small water crafts with them. They take them into the caverns and take them apart. I assume that they then sell them for parts."

"So, that's how that glidemobile gear ended up there," Sham commented.

"Excuse me?" Ryker didn't know what Sham was talking about.

"I found them in the cavern, Dad," Eli explained. "That's how Calli broke her ankle. They didn't know how to get out."

"Your son is a real hero," Gren said.

Ryker smiled. "That I believe." He looked at the boy. "It wasn't the smugglers this time, but they're due anytime now. You be careful."

"I will, Dad."

"So, how did you end up here?" Calli asked. "On this island?"

"A couple of orbits ago we went for a water craft ride," Ryker explained. "It was a beautiful morning, and we decided to spend a few rotations out on the open sea. We wanted to celebrate Eli's placement into the Mechanical Academy. There was a freak storm, and we crashed. Our water craft was all but destroyed. We've been living here ever since." He paused. "My wife doesn't know that we're still alive." Ryker swallowed hard to maintain his composure. "What about you? What's your story?"

Sham looked at Titus. "Captain Titus didn't check the fuel cell before we left and it was faulty."

"It shorted out," Titus explained. "I thought that the man who owns the craft would have checked it before we left, but I guess he didn't. But back at the Dream Wandering Learning Center they knew where we were headed, so if they study the map they should be here to rescue us soon." He glanced at Eli and smiled. "All of us."

Father and son exchanged a quick look. "You think they're going to find you if they study the map?" Ryker asked.

Titus nodded.

"Um," Ryker started slowly, "I don't really know how to say

this, but this is an uncharted island. That's why the smugglers like it so much. If your friends back home look only at a map, they'll never find us."

Titus' face fell. He had been counting on Ladinda and Ward finding them, based on the map. "Hold on a micro," he said. "We have a map in the supplies. Maybe it's been updated."

"I'll get it," Lawson said. He ran over to the supplies, grabbed the map, and handed it to Titus.

Titus moved so that he was sitting next to Ryker. "This is where we left from," he explained as he pointed. "Our fuel cell gave out when we were about here." He pointed again. "So, we drifted to this island, here."

Ryker shook his head. "That's not this island. We're actually right about here." He pointed to a spot in the middle of the water. "Islands without a suitable place to dock don't make it onto the maps, because they don't want vessel owners to head to them. It's a stupid policy, one that has kept Eli and me here all this time."

"So, the Learning Center isn't going to find us," Titus mumbled.

"Your water craft is still in one piece, right?" Ryker asked.

Titus nodded. "But we scraped some rocks, and I was worried about the integrity of the hull."

"The hull is fine," Eli announced with his mouth full of food.

"How do you know that?" Angel asked.

Eli grinned. "I swam out and took a look a couple of rotations ago. I couldn't help myself, I was curious."

"Was it just the fuel cell that you had problems with?" Ryker asked Titus.

"That, and our communications equipment. We had a short in the transmitter line, so we couldn't call for help."

"One of the few things that we were able to salvage from our water craft was the fuel cell," Ryker explained. "I don't know how much power is left in it, but it's worth a try. Eli and I will head out to your craft tomorrow and take a look. At the very least Eli might be able to do something with the transmitter. He's good with that kind of thing, which is why he was about to enter the Mechanical Academy."

Everyone agreed that it sounded like a great idea.

After the meal Ryker and Eli said that they were going to head back to the part of the island where they stayed. "Are we really going to get to go home, Dad?" Eli could be heard asking as they walked away.

"Don't get your hopes up too high, Son, but there's finally a chance," was Ryker's reply.

As the rest of the group settled down for the night, there was a new wave of optimism. Since it had been a long rotation, everyone fell right to sleep.

The whole group was up early the next morning. They gathered around where they usually made the fire, but they did not start one. Sham kept stretching and rubbing his shoulders, it was obvious that he was sore. "I'm sorry," Calli said.

"I'll be fine," Sham said with a grin. "In fact, I think that I'm going to make carrying you on my back a part of my new workout routine, even after your ankle has healed."

"Think again," Calli replied.

Less than a unit later Ryker and Eli arrived. Ryker had something in his arms, and Eli was carrying the missing blanket. There was something in it. "I brought back the rest of the food that I stole," Eli said quietly. "I'm sorry."

"No apology necessary," Gren said quickly. "We all understand."

"Still," Ryker said, "he shouldn't have done it. I've taught him better than to take things that don't belong to him."

"I also have the analyzer and the water bottle that you dropped when you disappeared into the cavern," Eli said. He put the blanket and its contents down. "We don't want the smugglers to find those and know that someone else has been here."

"When we get back home, Kid," Lawson said as he looked at the food, "we're going to take you to the finest restaurant on Terra. You can order anything you want, my treat."

"He's never offered to take me to the finest restaurant on Terra," Gren whispered to Calli.

"Let's work on actually getting off of this rock first," Ryker suggested. "Titus, since you know the craft the best you should come with us. Where's your lifeboat?"

"We don't have one," Titus replied.

Ryker looked at him. "You don't?"

"It's not my vessel, and we were only supposed to be gone a few units," Titus explained. "When we got here, we all swam to shore."

"It's okay, it's not that far," Ryker said. He looked at his son. "Are you up for a swim?"

"Sure, Dad."

"You up for this too, Titus?" Ryker asked. Titus nodded. "Good. Let's get going. The sooner we leave, the sooner we'll know if this is going to work. Titus, stick close to me. This fuel cell is not going to be an easy thing to swim with, and I may need you to take it for a little while."

∘ ∘ ●◯● ∘ ∘

After Ryker, Titus, and Eli were out of sight Calli turned towards her former partner. "Tayo, any chance you could help me for a micro?"

"What do you need, Kiddo?" Sham asked quickly. "I'll take care of you."

Calli smiled. "Sham, I truly appreciate all that you've done for me, but you are not taking me over to the girls' necessary area."

"I've got her, Sham," Tayo said. She lifted Calli onto her back and the two went away from the rest of the group.

Calli watched behind her and waited until she was pleased with their distance from the others. "Tayo, put me down. We need to talk."

"Why, what's up?" Tayo stopped and slowly let go of Calli.

"I'll probably get in trouble for telling you this, but everyone else already knows. Everyone but the kids, and I guess Ryker. But you really deserve to know."

"Know what?"

"This whole trip...it's been another one of Ladinda's trials. And Titus has been in on it all along."

"Titus set us up?"

Calli nodded.

"Why that little..."

"There's more," Calli continued. "Titus had been in contact with Ladinda, she had been wandering him, until a couple of rotations ago. Sham caught him doing it, so Titus told him what was going on. Then when I disappeared I guess that Sham told Gren, which is what started the fight between Sham and Titus, because Sham had promised that he wouldn't tell anyone. Or something like that. And then Sham told Lawson and me about it when we were in the cavern. Sham didn't think that it was a secret that should be kept from us, and I happen to agree with him."

"Wait..." Tayo was trying to let it all sink in. "So, whose trial is this? What is Ladinda trying to prove?"

"She wanted Angel and Dod to start getting along, and didn't care that she disrupted our lives in order to do it."

"So, does Ladinda know where we are?"

Calli shook her head. "I don't think so. Titus thought that she did, but I saw the look on his face when Ryker told him that this is an uncharted island. I think that we've been in the wrong spot all along."

"Wow." Tayo shook her head slowly, trying to mentally digest everything that she had just heard.

"We have an unspoken agreement to not tell Angel or Dod," Calli continued, "because otherwise this whole trip really was for nothing. The thing that gets me upset is that if Ladinda had asked us, we would have all gone along with it. She didn't need to keep the details from us."

"She must have had her reasons."

"Yeah, that's what I told Sham. He didn't buy it any more than I did."

"Speaking of Sham," Tayo said slowly, "you two seem to be getting along even better than normal."

"He saved my life." Calli thought for a micro. "Well, I guess that it was really Eli who saved my life, but Sham risked everything to find me. Tayo, I was so scared. I couldn't wander, no one was finding my dreams, and I was hurt so I couldn't even look for a way out. I had just about given up hope, then I heard Sham call my name. It was one of the most incredible micros of my life." She paused. "Just don't tell Sham that I said that."

"I won't."

"And we talked." Calli looked away, slightly embarrassed. "We're going to go out for dinner when we're back home. We want to see where this might lead."

Tayo grinned. "You don't have to convince me of anything. That's what Grey and I are doing. We're taking it slowly and seeing if maybe we do have a future together."

Calli laughed. "I'm taking it slowly. Sham keeps talking about our grandchildren." She decided that it was time to change the subject. "So, have you also noticed that something is off when it comes to wandering?"

"Yeah," Tayo replied. "The longer we've been here, the harder it's been. Remember that Declan once told us that certain atmospheric conditions can interfere with wandering distances. The wind picked up a couple of nights ago. I wonder if something else changed then as well."

"But it's not just distances. Sham and I tried wandering each other when we were stuck in the cavern. We were sitting as close to each other as you and I are right now, and we couldn't do it."

"It's probably just as well, you wouldn't want to know what Sham dreams about."

"Tayo, I'm serious! There's something strange going on here."

"I'm sorry, I couldn't resist."

"What really worried me," Calli continued, "was when Titus said that Ladinda had not been wandering him. If Ladinda can't wander, then it's more than an atmospheric condition caused by wind."

"Well," Tayo said, "we'll be going home soon. Titus, Ryker, and Eli will install the fuel cell, and then we can talk to Ladinda and find out what is really going on."

"Yeah, Ladinda always seems to have an answer for everything."

"Of course we're going to need to find a way to get you to Ward's water craft with your broken ankle," Tayo pointed out.

"If I have to swim through the pain I will," Calli said. "Whatever it takes to get back home. So...we should probably head back over and join the others. Can I have a ride?"

Tayo helped Calli to get onto her back. "Afraid that Sham is going to miss you?" she teased.

"Oh you be quiet," Calli replied.

Chapter Thirty-Six

Swimming to Ward's water craft was no easy task. The fuel cell was heavy and bulky. Titus had suggested that they carry it in a backpack, but even then it was not simple to swim with. Ryker and Titus switched who carried it several times during their short swim to the vessel.

Once they were on the water craft, Ryker asked Titus to show Eli where the transmitter was. "I can find the fuel cell on my own. But then come give me a hand."

Titus took Eli to the small craft's bridge. "I doubt that there's much that you can do with it," Titus told the young boy. "There was a power surge when the fuel cell failed and it fried the line, but it does have a backup power source."

"Well," Eli said, "I won't know if I don't try." It was wisdom that was beyond his orbits.

"True," Titus said.

Eli found a tool box and some wires. "I'm good with this sort of thing. That's why I was so excited to have been placed at the Mechanical Academy. I'll see what I can do."

"And I'm going to go help your dad."

As soon as Titus joined him Ryker closed the door. He stared at Titus for a moment. "So, what is it that you're not telling me?" Ryker kept his voice down. "I know that there's something that you don't want the younger ones to know. So, are you in some kind of trouble or something? On the run? Because your story just doesn't add up."

"No," Titus said slowly. "We're not on the run."

Ryker thought for a micro and then stared at Titus. "Those two kids, you didn't kidnap them, did you? Holding them for ransom?"

Titus shook his head. "No! It's nothing like that at all. Everything that we told you is true." He paused. "We just left out a few pieces of the story."

Ryker still looked suspiciously at Titus. "Like what?"

Titus lowered his voice. "You have to promise me that you won't tell anyone, not even Eli."

"I promise...unless what you say still makes no sense. This is my son that we're talking about."

"Fair enough. Ladinda...she's the woman who runs the Learning Center and is the most influential Dream Wanderer on the planet...she set us up so that we'd end up stranded."

"Why?"

"Angel and Dod are both very promising students, but they weren't getting along. Ladinda wanted to put them into a situation where they would have to learn to trust each other. She likes to go to extremes to make a point. We were only supposed to be here for a couple of rotations, and then they were supposed send someone to get us. The fuel cell failing was part of the plan. I was then supposed to drift, but I read the map wrong and we drifted to the wrong island. Ending up here wasn't part of the plan."

Ryker thought for a micro. "That's so crazy that it has to be true."

"Ladinda and I had been in contact through wandering," Titus continued. "But she hasn't wandered me in rotations, and we're all having problems wandering as well. We've become quite good at communicating through wandering, but for some reason we haven't been able to do it. Something strange is going on."

"I won't even pretend that I understand wandering," Ryker said, "but I do know a little bit about it. My brother saw a Wanderer a few orbits ago for a problem that he was having. The Wanderer really helped."

"Gren, Lawson, Sham, and I are all Apprentices who are going to be going through the Clinical Trials soon. That's what we need to do to get our licenses. Calli and Tayo are an orbit younger than we are and they're Apprentices as well. And Angel and Dod still have a long way to go in their studies. Wandering is a gift that someone is born with, but it takes orbits of schooling to learn how to actually do it. Plus there are a lot of laws regarding the practice, because wandering does mean invading someone's private thoughts. But see, we're not kidnappers or running from trouble. We're just a bunch of young adults who read a map wrong and got stuck on the wrong island."

Ryker laughed. "Well, let's see what we can do to get all of us off of the wrong island." He returned to his work on the fuel cell.

· · ●●◉●● · ·

"I wonder what's happening on the water craft," Gren said for the fifth time.

Lawson smiled. "They're probably putting the finishing touches on connecting the fuel cell, and then they'll swim back and tell us that we're ready to go home."

"How are we going to get Calli out there?" Angel asked.

"I'll take her on my back," Sham said.

"I'll be fine swimming on my own," Calli corrected. "But Sham will stay close in case I need help."

"I wonder how much longer it's going to take," Tayo added. They all wanted to know if they would soon be going home.

∘ ∘ ●◯● ∘ ∘

Eli ran down the stairs and threw the door open. "Dad, you'd better come quickly."

"What's wrong, Son?" Ryker asked. "Did you get the transmitter working?"

"I fixed the incoming, but you need to see something before I work on the outgoing. You too, Titus. You both need to see this."

Ryker and Titus followed Eli to the bridge. "I got the radar working as well. Look." He pointed.

Titus looked at the blip on the radar screen. "Maybe that's my friends from the Learning Center," he said. "They realized my mistake and are now looking in this direction."

Ryker shook his head. "That's not your friends, Titus. Look at the size of the ship. It's the smugglers."

Chapter Thirty-Seven

"I didn't want to work on the outgoing transmitter until I showed you that, Dad," Eli said.

"Good thinking, Son."

"Wait," Titus said. "If we have an outgoing line we can call for help."

"The smugglers would also be able to pick us up," Ryker explained. "They have their transmitter on, that's how we can see them on the radar. But they're not using it, they're listening for other signals. They're keeping their outgoing line on in case someone official comes along, it's the law. Once they get a little bit closer, they'll switch it off so that they can't be detected."

"But do you know for sure that the blip isn't someone from the Learning Center?" Titus asked.

"If that were a rescue vessel, they would have someone on the transmitter trying to contact you. Eli, you keep an eye on things here. See if you can fix the outgoing line but don't turn it on. Titus and I are going to try to do something with that fuel cell. We might need to get out of here in a hurry. Come on, Titus, it's time to get busy."

* * * * * * *

Even though Ryker had said that Titus was there to help, he felt like he was in the way. From time to time Ryker would ask for a tool, and Titus would hand it to him, but that was the extent of his usefulness. He was beginning to feel terrible about his part in the plan. If he had read the map correctly they wouldn't be in such a mess. Then again, finding the wrong island meant that Ryker and Eli could finally go home. At least something good would come of his mistake. Titus decided that he was going to apologize to Sham and the others. As much as he hated to admit it Sham was right, he should have let everyone know what was going on.

"Titus. Titus. Titus!" Eli's voice interrupted Titus' thoughts. "I said your name three times. Are you trying to wander or something?"

Titus shook his head. "No, just thinking about everything that's been going on. Anything new?"

"The smugglers are crossing over to the far side of the island. Your friends can probably see their vessel in the distance. Dad and I know where they dock, and then they'll use a water skimmer to get everything to shore. Have you ever seen a water skimmer, Titus?"

"In the distance and I've seen a few pictures."

"This thing is awesome! It just glides across the top of the water! The one that they use is gigantic. They'll sometimes load smaller skimmers onto it and then take those apart in the cavern."

The fuel cell needed to be attached in an enclosed area on the floor. Ryker pulled himself out of the small spot to join the conversation. "Any luck with the outgoing transmitter?"

Eli held up a mangled piece of wire. "This is all I've got to replace the burned-out wire with. I don't think I'm going to be able to do it. There's almost nothing in the emergency repair kit. It's almost like the owner of this water craft wanted you guys to get stranded." Titus and Ryker exchanged a quick glance. Eli didn't notice. "How is it going here?"

"Our fuel cell is providing its own set of challenges," Ryker replied. "Our craft was smaller, so the cell doesn't fit. I'm trying to get as much of a connection as I can, and then we'll have to hope for the best. I still don't know how much power is left in it."

Gren continued to try to wander. She couldn't pick anything up anywhere. There were no dreams to touch and no traces of tonic. Deep down, she was worried that the gift was gone.

Lawson sat next to her. "This is all going to be over soon," he said when she opened her eyes. "We'll be back home, and we'll be able to talk to someone about why we haven't been wandering. I'm sure that Ladinda will be able to explain it."

"Yeah, she has an explanation for everything." There was frustration in Gren's voice. "I don't like being upset with her, but I am." She paused. "Lawson, what if the gift is gone? What are we supposed to do then?"

"The chances of all of us losing the gift at the same time are ridiculously low." Lawson was trying to convince himself as much as he wanted to convince Gren. "And even if we did lose the gift, that's just our job. We still have each other." Lawson put his arm around Gren.

"Yeah, I know." Although she knew that Lawson was trying to make her feel better, she didn't feel comforted.

Angel and Dod had both taken off their shoes and they waded in the shallow water. "It's strange, but a part of me is almost going to miss this place," Dod said.

"I know what you mean," Angel agreed. "There's so much pressure on us back at the Learning Center. Here..."

"There's a different kind of pressure. Sorry, I didn't mean to interrupt."

"That's okay." Angel laughed. "Those were the exact words I was going to use."

"I like the water," Dod said. "Since we've been here, whenever I've started to get worried about something, all that I've had to do is to look out at the water and it's calmed me down."

"I know what you mean." Angel paused. "Hey, maybe when we're back at the Learning Center, we should spend more time by the lake. Gren and Lawson said that they were there all the time when they were students, and they turned out okay. Well, mostly okay."

"I'd like that." Dod stopped walking and stared towards the ocean. "Do you see that?"

Angel stood right next to him and stared. "What?"

Dod pointed. "Way off in the distance. There's something huge moving out there."

"Oh my goodness, Dod, you're right. There is something out there."

"We should tell the others."

"Eli, give me a hand. I want you to take a look at this." Ryker got out of the way and Eli slid into the small, enclosed space.

Almost a hundred passed before Eli's face could be seen again. "Do you think that's going to hold, Dad?"

"I hope so. I guess we'll know soon enough."

"Hey, everyone, come here!" Angel and Dod screamed in unison.

Gren, Lawson, and Tayo hurried to the water's edge to see

what was going on. Sham picked Calli up in his arms and carried her so that she could join them as well. Her ankle looked terrible, but she wasn't complaining. Sham was worried about how they would get Calli to the water craft if the fuel cell worked.

"What's up?" Lawson asked.

"Look!" Dod pointed. A shape could be seen in the distance.

"I wonder if they're from the Learning Center," Tayo stated.

"Would they send something that big?" Lawson asked. "I know we can't see it too well, but that ship looks huge."

"Well, wherever they're from, it's the first vessel that we've seen since we've been stranded," Gren added.

"You think they've realized that we read the map wrong?" Angel asked.

"I feel bad about that," Dod said quickly. "I was the one who found the island on the map. I was supposed to be the navigator."

Sham shifted Calli slightly in his arms. "You found the right island," he said. "It was our captain who had us drift to the wrong place."

"Well, whatever that ship was, they're almost out of sight," Gren pointed out.

"I wonder what's going on with Ryker and Eli," Sham said. He purposely didn't mention Titus.

"We'll know soon enough," Calli said. "And Sham, you can put me down anytime now."

"We need to go back and tell the others," Ryker said. "They'll want to know what's going on." He jumped into the water first, and was followed by Eli and Titus. They started the swim back to shore.

◦ ◦ ◐●◑ ◦ ◦

Even though the large ship was no longer in view, everyone stayed by the water's edge. Sham eventually put Calli down and sat next to her in the sand. "That ankle looks worse than it did when I found you."

"There was almost no light in there," Calli reminded him. "You couldn't see it well."

"Is that going to affect your work when we get back home?" Sham asked. "Do you meet the clients before you wander them?"

"I don't wander too many clients, not yet," Calli explained. "Declan lets us observe, and we spend a lot of time working on the simulator. So, I don't think that it will be a problem."

"Cassidy is more hands-on than that," Sham said. "She had Titus and me wandering within a couple of lunar cycles after we started to apprentice."

"Are you ready for the Trials?" Calli asked.

"The Trials," Sham repeated. "It's funny, I've hardly thought about them in rotations. Cassidy says that I'm ready, although she doesn't know about this problem that we've had wandering."

"I like Cassidy," Calli commented. "She's open to different ideas and approaches. I bet that she'll know why we haven't been able to wander, and she'll also know what to do to get the gift back."

"I hope so." Sham paused. "So...about our first date, when do you want to go?"

"How about after the Trials?" Calli suggested. "That way, you won't have what's coming up on your mind."

Sham smiled. "Believe me, Kiddo, when we're on our date I'm not going to be thinking about the Trials."

"Not even to tell me what they consist of?"

"Calli," Sham said with a laugh, "you're the most charming

person that I know, and I'm thrilled that we're going to give our 'it' a chance. But you're not going to be able to get any information about the Trials out of me. You'll have to wait your turn."

Calli grinned. "It was worth a shot."

∘ ∘ ⦾ ⬤ ⦾ ∘ ∘

Tayo decided to gather up their supplies. She used the waterproof containers to pack up the food, including some of the roots that they had found on the island. They had no idea how long they might be out on the water; assuming that Ryker and Eli would be able to get the fuel cell to work. She tried not to get her hopes up. "Hey Tayo," she heard Lawson call, "it looks like they're coming! We can see them in the water!"

"I'll be right there!" she called back. She finished what she was doing and joined the rest of the group. Three figures could be seen in the water. It didn't take them long to arrive.

"Any luck?" Lawson asked immediately.

"We got the fuel cell running," Eli explained, "but it doesn't have a lot of power left, and the connection is bad because it's the wrong size. I also got the incoming transmitter and the radar to work, but I didn't have enough spare wire for the outgoing."

"We need to leave immediately," Ryker added. There was an urgency in his voice.

"Why?" Sham asked.

"The smugglers are back," Ryker explained. "There's no telling what they'll do if they realize that someone else is here. I've overheard some of their conversations, these men are dangerous. Let's gather up the supplies and go."

Chapter Thirty-Eight

They wanted to make it look as if no one had been there, so the group got to work. Gren and Lawson destroyed the area where they had made their fires, trying to make it look as natural as possible. Tayo and Titus covered over what they had used as the necessary areas. It was not a fun job, but someone needed to do it. Sham and Ryker took care of the supplies. Angel, Dod, and Eli used branches to get rid of footprints and other signs that there had been people on the beach. Calli sat close by, keeping an eye on the children.

"I don't understand why we need to make it look as if no one was here," Angel said. "I mean, So, what if the smugglers see this? We'll be gone."

"I was thinking the same thing," Dod added. "They can't do anything to us if we're not here."

"They can come after us," Eli reminded his new friends. "They don't know how much we know. They're not going to take a chance that we can lead the System Workers back here."

"Oh," Angel and Dod said in unison.

Once the beach looked untouched, it was time to leave the island. The swim to Ward's water craft was not an easy one. Everyone, with the exception of Calli, had at least one waterproof container that contained food, drinkable water, or another supply that they had taken to shore. Calli swam on her back and tried to move her feet as little as possible. The pain was incredible, but she knew that she had to push past it. Sham stayed close, ready to help her if she needed assistance. She was determined to do it on her own.

Once they arrived at the craft, Titus and Ryker climbed up the rope ladder. They had left it down when they were there earlier. The kids were next, followed by Gren and Tayo. Sham grabbed hold of the ladder and positioned himself so that Calli could get on his back. Climbing the ladder and making sure that her ankle did not hit the side of the craft was not easy, but they made it. Lawson stayed in the water, and Ryker rejoined him. Titus climbed partway down the ladder and the three of them worked to hand the supplies to Sham, who was up on the deck.

Once everyone was on board and seated, Ryker and Titus went to start the water craft. The whole group breathed a collective sigh of relief when they realized that it had started. The vessel had been loud when they were on it the first time, but this time the engine almost seemed like a whisper. Gren thought that the gentle hum was one of the most beautiful sounds that she had ever heard.

Titus reappeared. "Ryker is going to keep an eye on the fuel cell," he explained. "Since it doesn't fit, he wants to be able to work on it immediately if there's a problem. Eli, Dod, do you two want to come help me at the controls?" Both boys nodded and stood up.

"Can I help too?" Angel asked.

"Of course," Titus replied. He and the three children headed towards the craft's bridge.

Calli sat with Tayo on her right side and Sham on her left. Tayo had found something that Calli could use to elevate her ankle. It hurt even more than it did when she first broke it.

"You doing okay?" Sham asked.

Calli nodded. "I'm trying. Although I will admit that I can't wait to have someone take a look at this thing and then give me something for the pain."

"If you want, I can talk to Cassidy. See if she'll give me some time off and then I can take care of you while you heal."

Tayo laughed. "Sham, she has me. Her roommate and best friend, remember?"

"And you live over two units away," Calli added.

"Oh yeah."

"Of course," Tayo continued, "if you want, you can come visit for a couple of rotations. You and Grey could ride together. I'm sure that Grey's former partner would let you stay with him. He's a nice guy, you'll like him. He and Grey have similar personalities."

"I think I'll pass."

"Besides," Calli said, "as soon as we're home you need to concentrate on getting ready for the Trials. The last thing that you need to do is to take more time off from work."

"If we still have the gift," Sham mumbled. He hoped that Gren hadn't heard him.

"Hey look!" Gren cried. She didn't seem to have noticed Sham's comment. "We're finally moving!"

Everyone watched as the island that they had been stranded on for several rotations seemed to grow smaller. They were going home. It was a great feeling.

Eli was thrilled to finally be leaving the island. As the craft headed out towards the open water, he wiped a tear from his eye. "Are you okay?" Angel asked.

The young boy nodded. "I thought that my dad and I would be there for the rest of our lives. I'm finally going home. I'll get to see my mom again, my grandparents, my friends. I hope that I can still attend the Mechanical Academy, but if I can't, that's okay. I'll get to sleep in a bed, eat real food, and wear new clothes." He wiped away another tear. I can't believe that we're finally off of that island."

● ● ●●● ● ●

Ryker wanted to be excited about returning home, but he knew that he needed to concentrate on making sure that the fuel cell didn't fail. If it did, they could end up in a worse situation than what they had just left behind. He was also worried about what he would find back home. He was sure that he and Eli had been legally declared dead. Life went on for his wife and everyone else. He was nervous about what his spot in the lives of his loved ones might be.

The lack of the engine's hum brought Ryker back into the micro. He checked the fuel cell and realized that the poor connection was draining power quickly. It wouldn't be enough for them to get back home. They would be lucky to have enough fuel for another two units. He also knew that going back to the island was not a good idea, especially since the smugglers had returned. "The smugglers!" he said out loud. It suddenly became crystal clear to him what they needed to do. He ran up to the deck. "Titus, Eli, come close enough so that you can hear," he called.

"What's going on?" Sham asked.

Ryker stood at the bottom of the stairs. "Can you guys hear me?"

"Yeah, Dad," Eli called back.

"Listen closely," Ryker started loud enough so that everyone could understand. "The fuel cell doesn't have enough power. If we keep going like this, we're going to end up drifting in the middle of the ocean. Without an outgoing transmitter, that's a risk that we can't take. But I have an idea on how we're going to get home."

"How?" Lawson asked.

"We're going to take the smugglers' ship."

Chapter Thirty-Nine

When Eli heard what his father said he rushed down the stairs. "Dad, we've talked about that before. We agreed that it would be too risky."

"That's because we never had a good way to get to their ship before," Ryker explained. "They dock where we couldn't swim to it without being seen, and they keep a guard by their water skimmer so that it won't wash out to sea."

"So, what's different this time?" Lawson asked.

"With this craft, we can approach their ship from the other side," Ryker explained. "Quietly. We'll get on board and take off before they know what happened. Plus we have more people to pull it off."

"Won't they come after us in the skimmer?" Gren asked.

"Probably. But those things are short distance. They're not made for deep water. If they go too far out in a skimmer, they're going to end up in trouble."

"How do we know that they don't have a guard on their ship?" Sham asked.

"We don't." Ryker paused. "But we do have the element of surprise. If there is someone watching things on their ship, he's going to be on the bridge, keeping an eye on the radar. Because we don't have outgoing transmissions, we won't show up on their screen. So, what do you guys say? Should we take their ship and go home? Or should we go back to the island and wait for a rescue that is never going to happen?"

"Let's do it!" Lawson said. Everyone else agreed.

· ·● ● ● ● ● ·

The plan was simple. The area where the smugglers docked was secluded, so if the group approached from the far side they would be able to get right next to the ship without being seen from shore. Once they had control of the smugglers' ship, they would attach a tow cable to Ward's water craft. "We can't leave it behind because the smugglers have access to fuel cells," Ryker pointed out. "It would be easy for them to change the cell and come after us. We want them stranded. Once we're home, we'll contact the System Workers."

The only problem in the plan was Calli. It would be difficult transferring her from one craft to the other without causing further injury to her ankle. "Why don't I just stay here?" Calli asked. "If you'll be towing the craft anyway, there's no reason for me to leave."

"I'll stay with her," Sham said immediately.

Calli shook her head. "Ryker is going to need you to help secure the smugglers' vessel."

"I'll stay with her instead," Tayo said quickly. "I know the basics of the controls. I may not be licensed like Titus is, but I can read the radar if needed and monitor incoming transmissions."

"That's a good idea," Calli said. "Tayo can keep an eye on me. She's been doing it for orbits."

Sham leaned close to Calli and kept his voice down. "Are you sure you don't want me to stay here?"

"They need you," Calli whispered back. "Besides, Sham, you're very close to smothering me. We agreed to take things slowly, remember?"

Sham smiled. "I thought we agreed to have grandkids."

Calli took Sham's hand. "Just be careful, okay?"

Sham winked. "Of course. I've got a lot to look forward to once we're back home."

• ◦ ● ● ● ◦ •

The smugglers had turned off their outgoing transmissions, so their ship no longer appeared on the radar. Ryker took over the controls of Ward's water craft, even without the radar he knew where to go. He was able to navigate so that they were right next to the smugglers' ship. He cut the power as they grew closer. They didn't know if any of the smugglers had stayed behind, and they wanted to make a silent approach. It had already been decided that Ryker would be the first to board, followed by Lawson, Gren, Titus, and Sham. All three children protested, but their cries were ignored. They were told that they would be able to board as soon as the adults had control of the ship. It was decided that Eli should watch the transmitter. He had to be prepared to move the ship immediately, if there was trouble.

Ryker maneuvered as close to the ship as he could. It was huge. Titus dropped the anchor when instructed. Everyone waited for a hundred, they seemed to be undetected. Getting to the smugglers' ship was not going to be simple. They secured one end of the rope ladder to the side of Ward's craft. Ryker used it to lower himself into the water. He then found a place to climb onto the smugglers' ship while holding the other end of the ladder. It wasn't easy, and he was obviously in good shape. He secured the ladder and silently motioned for the others to join him. Crossing on the rope ladder was difficult as well. Lawson went first. He slowly walked across the ladder, almost losing his balance several times. Gren was next. She realized that it would be easier to crawl than to walk standing up like Lawson had done. It took her less time. "Showoff," he mouthed to her once she was on the other side. Sham and Titus agreed that Gren's way was easier than Lawson's, so they crawled as well.

"We'll break into groups and search," Ryker whispered after everyone was safely across. "I'll check the bridge and the upper level. Gren and Lawson, you take the two lower levels. Sham and Titus, you search the middle two." The others nodded in agreement. "We'll meet back here in ten hundreds. Sound good?" They nodded again. "Okay. Good luck, and be careful."

Gren and Lawson started by searching the lowest level. It was where the smugglers kept their cargo. They discovered four whole glidemobiles, including a black one. They both knew that black glidemobiles were fairly rare and expensive. They also found an empty area that looked like a storeroom of some type. There were shelves along the walls. The two Apprentices assumed that they were in the room where the smugglers would store the parts after they had taken the glidemobiles apart. They finished their search and went to join the others.

Sham wasn't thrilled about searching with his former partner, but he wasn't going to let a grudge keep them from going home. There were two levels that they searched. They found food, clothes, and a few weapons, among other things. They decided that they should each take one weapon, just in case there was a problem.

When Sham and Titus were done, they headed back to meet Ryker. He was waiting for them. He wasn't alone.

Chapter Forty

Ryker was on his knees with his hands behind his head. The smuggler had a long weapon pressed into Ryker's neck. He noticed that both Sham and Titus had weapons of their own in their hands. "I'd suggest that you put those down, unless you want your friend here to meet an early death."

Titus and Sham did as instructed. "We don't want any trouble," Sham said.

The smuggler laughed. "Too bad, because you found it. Hands up, and move over here so I can see you better." Sham and Titus slowly moved next to Ryker. "Get down, just like he is. And don't even think of making any sudden moves."

Sham and Titus did as they were told. "You okay?" Titus asked Ryker.

"Yeah. Sorry about this, guys. He was on the bridge. I should have been more careful."

"Hey, no talking! Now, I just need to figure out who you are. Before I kill you, that is."

"If you're going to kill us, then we're not going to tell you who we are," Ryker said calmly. "You won't know if we're acting alone, or if we have an entire army coming at any micro."

The smuggler looked Ryker over. "I think I know who you are. Your clothes are worn and it's obviously been a long time since you've shaved. A couple of orbits back there were pieces of a wreck on shore, and every now and then we found signs that someone was living on the island. We talked about hunting you down and killing you, but we decided to let you be. And you repay us by trying to steal our ship?"

"If you had been marooned for orbits and you thought you had found a way home, wouldn't you take it?" Ryker asked.

The smuggler moved the weapon away from Ryker and pointed it in Titus and Sham's direction. "It's you two that I'm not sure about. What are you doing here on my vessel?"

"Same thing as him," Sham explained. "We kind of got stuck."

"There haven't been any bad storms since the last time we were here," the smuggler said. "So, what really happened?" He pointed the weapon at Titus.

"It wasn't a storm," Titus replied nervously. "Our fuel cell was faulty. When it blew, it shorted out our transmitter line. We drifted, and ended up on the island." He figured that it was best to stick to the truth, but leave out a few important pieces of information. He knew Sham well enough to know that he would realize what he was doing.

"A faulty fuel cell? You didn't check it before you left home?" The smuggler didn't seem to buy the story.

"Captain Titus didn't think to check," Sham said.

"Hey, I thought that it was fine! Ward said that he had looked everything over before he let me borrow his craft."

"But you were responsible for both of our lives," Sham argued. "You are the one with the license, you're supposed to double check everything!"

"You know, Sham, I'm getting really tired of you blaming this whole situation on me! You could give me a little bit of credit. After all, I did find a safe place for us to wait to be rescued."

"You found an uncharted island! How are we supposed to be rescued from that? You also forgot to let down the anchor, so we watched the craft just drift away. And look how safe we are now. Somehow I don't really feel safe with a weapon pointed at us."

The smuggler let Sham and Titus argue. It amused him, and he thought that maybe he could learn something about why they were really there as they fought.

Since they had finished their search, Gren and Lawson headed towards the designated meeting spot. As they walked closer, they could hear something off in the distance. "Sounds like Sham and Titus are fighting again," Lawson commented.

"Wait." Gren put out her arm and stopped Lawson from continuing forward. "Something's not right. Listen."

"And look how safe we are now. Somehow I don't really feel safe with a weapon pointed at us," Sham could be heard saying.

"They got caught," Lawson whispered. "And they're fighting to distract whoever it is who caught them."

"I wonder if Ryker is with them."

Gren listened for another micro. "We have to assume that he is. If we can get to the bridge, we can turn on the transmitter and try to call for help. I hope that Sham and Titus can keep the argument going."

"The way that they've been lately, it shouldn't be a problem."

At first Ryker thought that Sham and Titus really were arguing, but he soon realized that it was an act. With the fight they could warn Gren and Lawson of the danger, and it would also keep the smuggler from knowing about Ward's water craft. Sham had been smart to lie that the craft had drifted away. The smuggler seemed amused by the quarrel. The longer the man let them argue, the better.

On Ward's water craft Eli kept a close watch on the radar. It had a backup power source, so it didn't matter that the fuel cell was failing. He also listened to incoming transmissions. He wanted to be on the smugglers' ship with his father, but he understood why his dad had told him to stay behind. He couldn't wait until they were finally home again. He wondered what was taking so long.

Gren and Lawson quietly ran up to the ship's bridge. They agreed that the first thing that they needed to do was to turn on the transmitter. That way, the ship would be visible on radar if there was another vessel in the area. The controls were a lot more complicated than they expected them to be. After Lawson pressed several buttons, the transmitter turned on. "Easy," he said.

Gren watched what she thought was the radar. "There's nothing else on the screen," she remarked.

"We still need to try." Lawson picked up what he hoped was the microphone and pressed a button on the side. "If anyone can hear me, we need help. I repeat, if anyone can hear me, we need help. We're stuck on an uncharted island and we think that there are smugglers here. One of them has captured my friends. Please send someone to assist us immediately." He let go of the button. "How was that?"

"Good. Keep at it, we have no idea how far that thing will transmit. I just hope that the smuggler doesn't see Ward's craft. If Eli heard that, he'll know what to do."

· ᵒ ●●○ ᵒ ·

At first Eli was excited when he saw the smugglers' ship on the radar, but then he heard the transmission. He ran down the stairs. "They're in trouble," he told the others. "I heard someone calling for help, I think it was Lawson. He said something about his friends being captured. We need to get this craft hidden immediately."

"Do you know how to control this thing?" Tayo asked. Eli nodded. "Okay, you take care of that. We'll drop the ladder and pull up the anchor."

Eli ran back to the bridge, while Tayo, Angel, and Dod took care of everything else. Calli sat helplessly on the side and watched. She was nervous for all of her friends, especially Sham.

· ᵒ ●●○ ᵒ ·

"And I have no idea what Cassidy is going to say when we get back!" Sham said. "We've probably lost our jobs over this. She gave us only a couple of rotations off. She is not going to be happy."

"Cassidy is not going to fire us because we got shipwrecked! She'll understand."

"She'll understand that you didn't check the fuel cell? She is not going to want someone with so little intelligence working for her."

"Okay, enough!" the smuggler yelled. "I have no idea who Cassidy is and I don't care."

"She's our boss," Sham explained. "She's a Dream Wanderer, and we're her Apprentices. We're going to be going through the Trials soon, and..."

"Don't care," the smuggler repeated. "But there is one thing that I do care about. How come his clothes are wet," he pointed at Ryker, "and yours aren't?"

"He swam here," Sham said. "But Titus and I took the water skimmer. Man, that's a nice ride. It's too bad that you and your friends are taking them apart."

"Lucan was guarding the skimmer," the smuggler said.

"Lucan?" Sham repeated. "Is that the name of the guy who was sleeping on the beach? He didn't even notice us. We slipped right past him."

"That sounds like Lucan," the smuggler mumbled.

"We then let the skimmer drift," Titus added. "I know that we should have tethered it, but we were so excited about the idea of getting home that we weren't thinking straight." Titus hoped that the smuggler would buy his explanation of why the skimmer wasn't there. He also did not want to take a chance that the smuggler would look over the edge of the ship and see Ward's water craft.

Eli expertly piloted the craft away from the smugglers' ship. He kept close to the island, he didn't want to be too far from his father and the others. He was worried, but he knew that he needed to concentrate on what he was doing. It was up to him to take care of everyone on the small craft. He listened intently to Lawson's call for help, looking for more clues about what was going on. There was a small inlet that was well hidden by trees. He decided that it would be a good place for them to hide.

The view from the bridge was incredible. Gren could see as Ward's water craft slowly moved away. "Look," she said to Lawson. She pointed. "It looks like Eli picked up on what you were saying."

Lawson breathed a sigh of relief. "I didn't want to come right out and give instructions, just in case someone on the island also has a transmitter."

"Good idea."

"I'm going to keep calling for help." Lawson pressed the button on the microphone again. "If anyone can hear this, we need help..."

"Now I just need to take care of the three of you," the smuggler said. "Any volunteers on who wants to die first? Scrap that, I don't want to listen to you two argue any longer." He paused and scrunched up his face. "Wait a micro." He listened. In the distance he could hear a voice. "Holy splarsh, you're not alone, are you? You've got someone calling for help!"

"I don't know what you're talking about," Sham said.

"Up, all three of you!" The smuggler's voice had changed, it was filled with anger. The three of them stood up. "We're going up to the bridge to meet your friend. You'll go first because you know the way," he pointed the weapon at Ryker, "and you're second." He pointed it at Titus. "And you'll be right in front of me." He waved the weapon in Sham's face. "Line up, now." They got into a line and started to walk towards the stairs. "We're going to do this real quiet like. Everyone keep their hands on their heads, and don't even think of pulling something. If you do, the skinny one here gets it."

"The skinny one?" Sham mumbled to himself. He knew that Titus would never let him live that down...if they were to make it off of the ship alive.

Chapter Forty-One

As they climbed up the stairs towards the bridge the only thing that Sham could think about was finding a way to warn Lawson, whose voice could still be heard in the distance. Sham knew that starting another fight with Titus at that micro was out of the question, it was too obvious. He thought of something simple, something that the smuggler might believe. He knew that he was taking a huge risk, but it would be worth it if he saved his friends.

Sham knew that timing was everything. If he waited until they were near the bridge, the smuggler might realize what he was doing. If he did it too soon, Lawson might not pick up on what was going on. When Ryker reached the top step, Sham listened. Lawson had paused, so Sham realized that the timing was as close to right as possible. He sneezed as loudly as he could.

The smuggler did not like the fact that Sham had made a noise, and jabbed the weapon into his back. "Ow!" Sham said loudly, which caused the smuggler to repeat the action. Sham turned around and whispered, "Sorry, a sneeze is just one of those things that you can't control." In the distance, Lawson could be heard on the transmitter once again. Sham realized that his plan had failed.

The bridge wasn't too far from the top of the stairs. The smuggler motioned for them to enter the area in the same order. Lawson was standing there, the microphone in his hand. "I suggest you drop that," the smuggler said, "unless you want to watch your friends here die." Lawson did as instructed. "Good. Now, hands up, and get in line next to the skinny one."

Lawson looked at Sham and then Titus, unsure which one the smuggler was talking about. He then went and stood next to Sham. "We don't want any trouble," Lawson said.

"Then why are you calling for help? That's going to bring me a whole lot of trouble." Keeping an eye on all four of them, he crossed the room and turned off the outgoing transmitter.

"We told the smuggler what happened," Titus said. "How we had a problem with the fuel cell and all that."

"'The smuggler'?" The man repeated. He laughed.

"Wait," Sham started, "are you a smuggler, or a pirate?"

Titus shook his head. "Sham, you don't know anything. A smuggler is someone who steals things and then takes them somewhere else to sell them, without paying the proper taxes and fees. A pirate is someone who attacks a ship out on the open sea, and then takes over the ship. Isn't that right?"

The smuggler laughed again.

"Sorry I'm not up on my criminal behavior, Titus," Sham shot back. "Maybe that's why Cassidy likes me better than she likes you. I spend my time actually working, not researching things that aren't going to make any difference."

"You don't know what you're talking about! I like to research, because I want to be well informed about what clients might have nightmares about!"

"And being attacked on the open sea is a top nightmare?"

The smuggler rolled his eyes and then grinned. Their fighting still amused him.

When Lawson's voice was no longer heard calling for help, Eli hoped that he was just taking a break. When the smugglers'

ship disappeared from the radar, Eli's heart sank. He knew that something was terribly wrong.

∘ ∘ ∘●∘ ∘ ∘

"I really can't wait until we've passed the Trials," Titus said loudly. "I'm going to find a practice that is far away from wherever you are!"

"Except for the fact that we're not going to make it to the Trials," Sham reminded him. "Because we're not going to make it out of this alive."

"You got that right," the smuggler added.

"And that's my fault?" Titus asked.

"You're the one who didn't check the fuel cell!" Sham exclaimed.

The smuggler laughed. "He's got a point."

"I didn't think that Ward would let me borrow a craft that he hadn't checked over."

The smuggler shook his head. "If you were captain of the vessel, you should have checked everything over yourself. Didn't you realize that the lives of your passengers were at stake?"

"So, Titus," Sham continued, "even our smuggler friend here realizes that you were wrong." He looked at the smuggler, who was obviously amused by the conversation. "What do you want us to call you? I mean, you're going to kill us, so it wouldn't hurt anything if you told us your name."

"You can keep referring to me as 'the smuggler' if you want."

"Okay," Sham said, "we'll do that."

"What I don't understand," the smuggler said, "is why you two even agreed to a water craft trip together, since you obviously hate each other."

"We don't hate each other," Titus said. "We've been best friends for orbits."

"We were best friends, until I agreed to this trip." Sham looked directly at the smuggler. "See, I've got the most beautiful girlfriend back home, and because of Captain Titus I'm never going to see her again."

"She's not your girlfriend," Titus reminded him.

"Not yet, but she would have been soon. We were going to have the most romantic first date in the history of Terra. But now, thanks to you, that's never going to happen."

"Romantic?" Titus laughed. "All that you and Calli do is poke each other in the arm!"

"And the problem with that is?"

As Sham and Titus argued, Gren slowly came out of her hiding place. She was directly behind the smuggler. She held in her hands a piece of equipment. She had no idea what it was for, but she did know that it was heavy. She lifted it as high as she could, then brought it down on top of the smuggler's head. He was instantly out cold.

"Took you long enough," Sham said.

Ryker immediately turned the outgoing transmitter back on. "Eli, if you can hear me, we're all fine. We've secured the ship, and we'll be out of here soon. We're going home, Son."

Sham and Titus worked together to tie up the smuggler. They then dragged him into a corner.

Lawson broke the smuggler's weapon into two pieces. "Good job," he said to Gren.

Gren was filled with adrenaline. "I needed to wait for the right micro. I didn't know if I had it in me."

Lawson smiled. "Gren, I'm now more convinced than ever

that you can do anything." He turned towards Sham. "Thanks for the sneeze. We never would have known that you were on your way up here otherwise."

Sham was happy to hear that his warning had worked. "You're welcome. But how did you know that I was the one who sneezed?"

"I've lived with you and Titus for orbits," Lawson said as if no further explanation was necessary.

○ ○ ○●○ ○ ○

When Eli saw the smugglers' ship back on the radar, he jumped to his feet. He turned up the incoming transmitter as loud as it would go. "Eli," he heard his father say, "if you can hear me, we're all fine. We've secured the ship, and we'll be out of here soon. We're going home, Son."

"They're fine!" he screamed down to the others. He hoped that it wouldn't take too long until the two crafts were together, and they were headed back out towards the open sea.

Chapter Forty-Two

It didn't take long to find Ward's water craft. Ryker maneuvered the smugglers' ship as close as possible. They found a plank, and used that to move back and forth between the two vessels. Although they still needed to be careful, it was easier to cross on the plank than it had been on the rope ladder.

Ryker and Titus attached one end of a tow line to the smugglers' ship, and then connected Ward's water craft. It was decided that Titus would stay on board and monitor the transmitter. He wouldn't be able to send any transmissions, but Ryker could keep him informed if there was anything that they needed to know. Calli and Tayo also stayed on Ward's craft. Calli's ankle looked worse than ever, and everyone agreed that she needed to stay off of it.

It took them less than half a unit to have everything ready. Ryker then slowly steered the ship out of the grove, and Ward's craft came with it. As the island disappeared from view, a moving water skimmer could be seen close to shore. There was no danger, skimmers were low water level vehicles and the smugglers would not be able to follow very far without running into trouble.

• ○ ○●○ ○ •

Out on the open sea Ryker was at the controls. It seemed to come naturally to him. Angel and Dod watched the radar, and Eli kept an eye on the smuggler. He was awake and he struggled to free himself of his bonds, but it was no use. He finally stopped squirming and instead passed the time by staring menacingly at

Eli. The young boy was not intimidated.

"Ryker, look!" Dod said excitedly. He pointed at the radar screen. "There's something out there!"

Ryker looked at the screen, then picked up the microphone. "It's a Sea Protectors' ship," he said. He took a deep breath. "Attention, Sea Protectors, if you can hear me, we need help. I repeat, we need immediate help."

"We can hear you," a voice replied. "What seems to be the problem?"

"My son and I were marooned a couple of orbits back. We've been living on an uncharted island. A few rotations ago a group from the Dream Wandering Learning Center ended up stuck on the same island. We were able to commandeer a ship from some smugglers, most of them are now stranded on the island. One of them is with us. We need assistance in getting back home."

"We're out here looking for the group from the Learning Center," the voice said. Are all eight of them with you?"

"Everyone is here," Ryker replied. "We have one minor injury, a broken ankle, but for the most part they're all healthy and in good shape. Their fuel cell failed and they also don't have outgoing communications. I'm towing their craft behind me, but without the transmitter you won't be able to see it on your radar."

"Got it. And what is your name?"

"Mine? I'm Ryker."

There was static on the other end for a micro. "Did you say 'Ryker'? And your son is Eli?"

"Yes, that's correct," Ryker replied.

"I remember your case," the voice said. "We searched for you for lunar cycles. We found some debris from your craft, and eventually it was declared that you died at sea. There are going to be some very happy people when they discover that you're still alive. Hold on one micro." There was more static. "I've contacted the System Workers on a private channel and informed them of the smugglers. We'll lead you back to shore."

"Thank you." Ryker put down the microphone and looked at Eli. "It's really happening, Son. We'll be home soon."

"Mom is going to be so happy to see us!"

Ryker nodded. He hoped that his son was right.

Once the dock was in view Ryker gave Titus instructions to drop the tow line and turn the craft back on. He did as he was told. It seemed like it took forever to dock. Two System Workers boarded the smugglers' ship and took the smuggler off. A medical team boarded the other craft to take care of Calli. She was the first one back on shore because she was wheeled off on a gurney. Everyone else slowly left the two vessels and walked up the docks. A few people could be seen in the distance, waiting for them. Gren immediately recognized Ladinda and Cassidy. There was a man there who she was pretty sure was Declan, and a woman that she did not recognize.

Eli saw the woman. "Mommy!" he screamed and ran into her waiting arms. The woman picked up the child and held him close.

Ryker wiped a tear from his eye. He had no idea what to expect. Still holding Eli, the woman started moving forward. Ryker took that as a good sign and ran to join his wife and son. They embraced, squeezing Eli in the middle. "I never gave up hope," his wife said. "I knew that we'd be together again."

Gren glanced at her friends. They were all crying. As she blinked away a few tears of her own she realized that maybe getting stranded was worth it after all. They had brought a family back together.

Chapter Forty-Three

It was decided that everyone should stay at the Medical Center for one night for observation. The parents of both Purples were contacted, and they met them at the Center. All of the Apprentices were able to speak with their loved ones as well to assure them that they were fine. Gren had to promise her mother that she and Lawson would come for a visit soon. There were a lot of questions from the System Workers and the Sea Protectors. They needed to know what had happened, and they also learned the location of the island. The group was assured that the rest of smugglers would soon be caught.

After a good night's sleep in real beds the group was evaluated one more time. Ladinda had made arrangements for transportation so that they could return to the Learning Center. Before they left, they needed to say good-bye to Ryker and Eli. Ryker was clean shaven and Eli finally had on clothes that fit. His mother stood between the two of them, holding their hands. She had received permission to spend the night at the Medical Center and she looked as if she never planned on leaving either of their sides again.

There were hugs and tears, and more than one comment about Eli's new shoes. Everyone promised to keep in touch. Ryker and his family waved good-bye, and then climbed into a glidemobile. They were finally returning home.

The trip back to the Learning Center flew by. They were all in the same vehicle, and the dynamic was quite different than it had been when they had headed towards the ocean. Angel and Dod sat next to each other; close, but careful to not touch. Gren and

Lawson exchanged a knowing glance, they remembered acting like that all too well. There was nonstop talk about everything from the new bandage on Sham's eye to whether or not Eli's mother would even consider letting him attend the Mechanical Academy. Several times Calli was asked how she was feeling. She was doing much better. Her ankle had a proper cast on it and she had been given something to numb the pain.

Ladinda greeted the vehicle when it arrived at the Learning Center. She dismissed Angel and Dod. They walked away together, talking. Ladinda then suggested that everyone have a meal, and after that they could all discuss what had happened. While they were eating they noticed that Angel and Dod were sitting together. Two Purple girls approached Angel and it was obvious that they tried to get her to sit with them elsewhere. Angel shook her head, and motioned for the girls to sit down there instead. They did. "That's promising," Gren commented.

"Or Dod just bought himself a whole lot of trouble," Sham said with a grin.

Once they had finished eating, the group headed towards Ladinda's office. They took it slowly because Calli was still getting used to the crutches. Titus motioned with his head for Sham to hang back behind the others. "Can we talk?"

"Yeah, what's up?"

Titus paused. "I just want to say that I'm sorry. You were right, I should have let you know what was going on. I hope that you'll eventually be able to forgive me, and that we'll be able to be friends again."

"I don't know," Sham started slowly. He then grinned. "Titus, I haven't been mad at you since we put on that fake fight for the smuggler. I realized then that we still make a good team. You have to admit, arguing like that was kind of fun."

"In a 'I don't know how we're going to make it out of this alive' sort of way."

"Exactly."

"I'm glad that we're okay again." Titus laughed. "If we weren't, I wouldn't be able to refer to you as 'the skinny one', and that's going to be such a fun thing to call you."

"Hey," Sham said, "if you even think of calling me that, this whole friendship is off again."

Ladinda didn't hold the meeting in her office. Instead, it was in a larger conference room. There was a circular table in the center with chairs all around it. Cassidy, Declan, Haas, and Hutch were there already. There was a pitcher of water in the center with glasses next to it. There was also a plate with snacks. "I thought that it would be more comfortable to have this talk in here," Ladinda said. She motioned for everyone to sit down. "Calli, how are you doing?"

"I'm managing okay, Ma'am," she replied. "I've never been on crutches before, so it's going to take me a little while to get the hang of them."

After everyone was seated Ladinda looked at the group in front of her. Even though there was no real head to the table, she seemed to be seated in the position that held the most authority. "First off, I want to thank all of you. Your time with Angel and Dod seems to have really helped them, there is an obvious improvement. This was a turning point in their education, and if they make it all the way through the program they will have you six to thank. Second, I need to apologize to you. I'm assuming that Titus told everyone about my plan?"

Sham raised his hand. "Ma'am, Titus didn't tell anyone, not willingly. I caught him when you were wandering him, and I knew that something was going on. He then filled me in because I wouldn't let it rest. I'm the one who told everyone else, with the exception of Tayo. I'm not really sure how she found out."

"I told her," Calli said quickly.

"We were very careful, Ma'am," Gren added. "We made sure that Angel and Dod never knew what was going on. As far as they know, Ward had no idea that he was sending us off in a craft with a faulty fuel cell."

"That's good to hear," Ladinda said. "They must never learn the truth. Sometimes it's okay to let a student know that he or she has gone through one of my trials, but in this case it would only hurt the progress that they've made. Usually my plans don't get as out of hand as this one did, and for that I am truly sorry. We had no idea that you were not on the island that Titus and I had originally talked about. When I couldn't wander him, I knew that something was wrong. I immediately sent the Sea Protectors to the correct island, and you obviously weren't there. They then started searching for you. I contacted Haas, Cassidy, and Declan to let them know what was going on. Cassidy and Declan both came to the Learning Center to try to find you through wandering as well. Hutch joined us, and the four of us tried nonstop to find some trace of one of your dreams, but we couldn't."

Haas held up a hand because he wanted to say something. "Gren and Lawson, I don't want you to think that I didn't help wander because I didn't care, because I did. I do." He paused, and looked around the table. "What I am about to say cannot leave this room." His stare stopped on Gren. "I didn't join the others because I can't wander distances. It's something that I never saw as practical, so I didn't take the time to learn. I still don't see how it would be practical in a clinical setting, but I do now understand that it is a good skill to know for an emergency situation."

Gren nodded but didn't say anything. She was surprised. Haas was considered by most to be one of the two best Dream Wanderers on the planet, and there was a wandering skill that she was better at than he was.

"The whole thing has given me an idea," Ladinda continued, "but now is not the time or place for that. As I was saying, we tried to find you through wandering, but we didn't have any success. I then remembered what Titus had told me about someone stealing your food. I knew that you had analyzers with you, and that you were probably eating something that was growing on the island." She held up a piece of paper. "This is your blood work from the Medical Center. All of you tested positive for farium oxitate. It is not something that is found in the foods that we eat here, so I had the different types of root vegetables that you brought back with you tested. One of them showed high amounts of farium oxitate as well." She looked around the table, none of the Apprentices seemed to understand what she was saying. "It's not widely known, but farium oxitate interferes with wandering. It will block the dream so that Wanderers can't find it. It happens gradually, it will first affect distances and then closer contact. The chemical also temporarily stifles the gift of wandering. That is why we weren't able to find you, and why you eventually couldn't even find each others' dreams. As soon as the farium oxitate is out of your systems, you'll be wandering like always. There are no long term effects."

All six Apprentices seemed relieved. They also suddenly understood why Calli was the first one who they couldn't wander. She had tried one of the root vegetables before any of the others, so she was the first one to have farium oxitate in her system. Calli had a question about something else so she raised her hand. "Declan, didn't you tell us that sometimes atmosphere can also interfere with wandering?"

Declan nodded. "It can. But it has to be an extreme condition. Just because it rains or the wind picks up does not mean that wandering will be affected." Calli nodded in understanding.

"Now," Ladinda said, "I'm sure that you all have questions and other things that you would like to discuss. Where should we begin?"

The session with Ladinda and the others lasted for almost two units. When it was over the six Apprentices just wanted to get back home. They found Angel and Dod and said good-bye to both of them. They then picked up their possessions from the Teachers' Building. Sham carried his things as well as Calli's. Ladinda and Hutch were in the parking area, waiting to send them off.

Ladinda called Gren over to the side, there was something that she needed to say. "Gren, there was another reason that I wanted you to help me out with this plan."

"What was it?"

Ladinda looked at Gren and smiled. "I know that you've been putting a lot of pressure on yourself because of the Clinical Trials. I wanted to get your mind off of them for a little while. You're extremely talented, my dear, and you have the potential for great things. Don't fret over the Trials. You're going to sail through, and once you're licensed, we'll talk again."

Gren was encouraged by the pep talk. "Thank you, Ma'am." She wasn't really sure why she was thanking Ladinda for disrupting her life yet again, but she was grateful for the boost.

Ladinda and Gren rejoined the group. Sham was standing next to Calli's glidemobile. "I can take you home. With that ankle, you can't operate a glidemobile."

"But Tayo can," Calli reminded him. "Sham, I promise you that I'll be fine." She gave him a kiss on the cheek. "We'll talk soon. Make it through the Trials, and then we'll celebrate. Okay?"

"Okay." Sham grinned. "Our grandkids are counting on it."

Calli loosened up her grip on one of the crutches so that her hand was free. She jabbed a finger into Sham's arm. "Poke."

There were more hugs and then everyone climbed into the two glidemobiles. It had only been a few rotation since they left home, but it felt like an eternity.

Chapter Forty-Four

It took a few rotations for the farium oxitate to completely leave their systems, and they were all relieved when they were able to wander and be wandered once again. Gren knew that she needed to turn her focus back to preparing for the Trials. She still had no idea what to expect. She also didn't know when the Trials would take place. Not knowing was the worst part.

One rotation when she and Lawson showed up for work Haas sent Lawson on an errand. He then instructed Gren to prepare for a session. She was always glad to have an opportunity to practice. When she arrived in the wandering room, there was no client. The only people there were Haas and Aribella. "You're ready, Gren," Haas explained. "It's time for your Clinical Trials."

Gren glanced around the room. Nothing was different or out of place. "I don't understand," she said nervously.

"It's quite simple, Gren. For the Trials, you'll be wandering me." Haas held up a small bottle. "This is a special tonic that will allow me to remember everything that happens. It will also, unfortunately, produce some rather unpleasant dreams. It's your job to guide me through the process. Aribella will observe. If her assistance is needed, you'll have failed. I doubt very much that is going to happen. After the session is over, Aribella and I will talk about what happened. She'll be able to give her opinions from a clinical aspect, while I'll be going more on emotions, how the session felt. We'll have your results before Lawson returns from his errand. Do you have any questions?"

Gren thought for a micro. She had waited her entire life for this, and her mind was racing. "How long does the session last?"

she asked.

"That depends on you, Gren," Haas said. "The faster you work out the problems, the sooner the session will end. But I'd advise you not to rush through it. Treat this like a regular session. Anything else?" Gren shook her head. "There's one more thing that I need to say. Lawson is going to experience his Trials this afternoon. I've done my best to keep the two of you apart this rotation, but if you do see him do not let him know anything about this. Understood?"

"Yes, Sir."

"Good. Let's get this over with." Haas downed the contents of the bottle and stretched out on the wandering table. "Relax, Gren. You're one of the most talented Dream Wanderers that I've ever seen. You'll be fine." Haas closed his eyes and Gren's Trials began.

Gren felt as if she was floating on air as she and Lawson walked home. They had both easily passed the Trials. They would receive their licenses in a ceremony in a few rotations. Lawson invited Gren over for the evening meal. He wanted to brag to Sham and Titus that they had both passed the test.

"Guess what!" Sham said as soon as Lawson opened the door. "Titus and I passed the Trials!" He noticed that Gren was standing behind Lawson. "Oh, hi, Gren. Sorry about that, I didn't realize that you were there."

Titus knew how stressed Gren had been about the Trials. "We of course can't tell you what happened, but Gren, you won't have any problems."

"I know. We passed too," Gren said with a smile.

"So, we can talk about it!" Titus said. "That's good, I thought that I was going to have to avoid you until Haas finally got around to it. Without the specifics, which would still be breaking the rules, what did you two have to go through?"

"Storms, shipwrecks, kidnappings, the usual," Lawson said.

Titus smiled. "Yeah, nothing we've never been through before."

"The worst part," Sham said, "was that Cassidy had Grey observe. My entire future was in his hands. Can you believe it?"

"You and Grey might not get along on a personal level," Titus said, "but he'll come through when needed. Even for you, Sham."

"Oh Gren," Sham started, "before I forget, I've invited Calli to come for the Licensing Ceremony. Tayo too. I told them that they can stay with you for a few rotations. I knew you wouldn't mind."

Gren rolled her eyes. "Of course I don't mind, but why will they have to stay for a few rotations? The ceremony will only last a unit or so."

"Sham thinks that he can finally talk Calli into going on that date with him," Titus explained.

"She's already agreed! She wanted me to concentrate on the Trials first. Now that I've passed, it's time for the next phase in my life to begin. I've got a new job, and soon Calli is going to be a big part of my life as well."

"Cassidy has offered us Associate Wanderer positions," Titus said.

"What about Haas?" Sham asked. He knew that it might be a sore subject, because of Haas' rules, but it didn't make any sense to ignore the topic.

"He didn't say anything about the future," Lawson replied.

"To either one of us," Gren added.

∘ ∘ ●◉● ∘ ∘

The Licensing Ceremony wasn't large, and was held at Haas' office complex. Gren, Lawson, Sham, and Titus were the only four Apprentices in their area who were about to receive their licenses. There was a small group of family and friends present to share in their special occasion. Calli's ankle was still healing, but she was much more comfortable on the crutches. There were some friends there that they hadn't seen in a long time. Sham's friend Roy was seated in the back with a woman named Fia. Both of them had played a huge part in their lives back when they were still at the Learning Center.

Ladinda didn't usually handle Licensing Ceremonies, but this one was special. She gave a small speech which mentioned how proud she was of all four of them. When it was time to hand out the licenses, Cassidy first gave them to Sham and Titus. She hugged each of them. When it was Haas' turn, he gave out hugs with the licenses as well. Hugging was something that he did not do very often, but the hugs came from his heart. He was truly proud of Gren and Lawson.

After the ceremony there was a reception, paid for by Haas. That was unlike him. Gren wondered if maybe his gruff exterior was mostly an act. She had seen some glimpses of his subconscious mind during the Trials. She suspected that maybe he did have a heart after all.

Gren knew that she needed to think about her future. Haas had not mentioned the possibility of an Associate Wanderer position to either her or Lawson, which meant that she no longer had a job. She knew that she needed to start looking for information on different practices and see where there were openings. She intended to keep her promise to Lawson. They were going to finally be together, even if it meant working apart.

Gren realized that her future could wait for a little while. All of her favorite people had gathered to celebrate her success, and she wanted to spend time with them.

• • •●● • •

While the reception was still going strong Haas asked Lawson to meet him in his office. Lawson looked around for Gren, she was talking to Ladinda. Part of Lawson was still slightly upset with Ladinda for what she had put everyone through, but he knew that Gren was more forgiving than he was. Lawson couldn't help but wonder why Haas wanted to speak to him, but not Gren. Maybe he planned to speak with her later. He probably did not want to interrupt Gren's conversation with Ladinda.

Lawson left the main group and walked down the hall to Haas' office. The door was closed, so he knocked.

"Come in." Lawson opened the door. Haas was seated behind his desk. "Lawson, Son, please close the door and have a seat."

"What can I do for you, Sir?" Lawson took a seat, and tried not to let his surprise show that Haas had referred to him as "Son".

"I wanted to have a little talk about your future," Haas explained. "Have you accepted an Associate position anywhere yet?"

Lawson shook his head. "No, Sir."

"Good. I never found a replacement that I was happy with for Thaddeus, so I have an opening, if you're interested."

"Thank you, Sir, but what about..."

"I can assure you that I pay handsomely," Haas continued. "I might even be willing to renegotiate your payback percentage. We can go over the details about that later."

"But Sir..."

"And you'll have your own office. I treat my employees very well. I know that you and Gren might not agree, but I never really considered either of you employees. Apprentices are there to learn, and learn you both did."

"Sir..."

"You'll work hard if you take me up on my offer," Haas continued, "but it's rewarding work. You'll also have prestige that you've never experienced before. I'm considered the best for a reason, and my Associates have a standard that they need to live up to."

"Sir..."

"I'm not expecting an answer right now. Think it over for a couple of rotations. Do you have any questions?"

"Yes," Lawson said immediately, grateful for a chance to speak. "What about Gren?"

"Gren is an extremely talented Wanderer," Haas said. "I don't think that she'll have a problem finding a suitable position. I'll be more than happy to write her a recommendation if she needs it, but I doubt that she will."

"What about a position for Gren here?" Lawson asked.

Haas shook his head. "I only have one opening. You have a better rapport with the children than Gren does. You're my first choice. Besides, even with Associates, my rules don't change. If you and Gren were to both work for me, you'd stay only friends. I'm not blind, Lawson, I know that you two have feelings for each other." Haas stared at Lawson. "Don't let a job get in the way of true love, Son."

"If I turn you down, would you offer the position to Gren?" Lawson asked.

Haas paused. "I don't know. I haven't thought about the possibility that you might turn me down. This is the chance of a lifetime, Lawson. You'll be able to work in the best Dream Wandering practice on Terra, and you and Gren will finally be able to be more than friends. You've worked hard for this opportunity, and you deserve it."

· · ●○●○ · ·

Lawson left Haas' office more confused than he had been in a long time. All during school he had never thought much about working for a prestigious practice, but he had mostly enjoyed his time as an Apprentice for Haas. He liked the idea of making good money at a practice that people respected. He was pretty sure that he wanted to take the job. He just didn't know how he was going to tell Gren.

When Lawson returned the the reception, goodbyes were being said. He thought that maybe that would buy him a little bit of time before having to tell Gren about his conversation with Haas. She saw him the micro that he entered the room and ran up to him. "Where have you been? I've been looking everywhere for you!"

Gren was obviously in a good mood, and Lawson hated the idea of ruining it for her. He decided that his news could wait. "I've just been thinking about the future." It wasn't a lie, but it also wasn't the whole truth.

"Speaking of the future," Gren said, "I have fantastic news. I wanted to share it with you first, I haven't even told my family yet."

"What's up?"

A smile spread across Gren's face. "Ladinda has offered me a job as a teacher at the Learning Center. She wants to start a class on distance wandering for Greens and Blues, and she thinks that I'm the perfect one to teach it. Isn't that incredible?"

Gren gave Lawson a hug, which he returned. He was wrong, Gren wasn't going to be upset about the possible position with Haas. What she had been offered was a dream come true for her. "That's wonderful," he whispered.

After several micros, Gren let go. "So, what about you? Are you going to take the Associate position with Haas?"

Lawson stared at his former partner and best friend. "How did you know about that?"

"Haas was missing too. Lawson, I'm so proud of you. It's up to you whether or not you take it, but you deserve it." She hugged him again. "We finally made it," she whispered in his ear.

Chapter Forty-Five

Gren only had a few rotations until she needed to leave. There was a teaching class at the Learning Center that Ladinda wanted her to take, since she had no formal training as a teacher. Ladinda didn't think that her lack of training would be a problem; Gren would be working with only two students at a time and she would be sharing information that she had taught her friends in the past.

As a gift for receiving her license, Gren's parents had bought her a glidemobile. Lawson helped her carry some boxes out to it. Since the dwelling where she had lived for the two previous rotations was furnished, she didn't have all that much to move. "Did you know that all of the teachers wander for free?" Gren asked her best friend. "There's a clinic that Ladinda started, and the teachers take turns working there. Ladinda wants them to keep up with practical experience in a clinical setting, and it's a nice way to give back to the community."

"It sounds like a great program," Lawson said. He failed to mention that Gren had told him about the clinic at least a dozen times over the past few rotations.

"I was glad when she told me about it," Gren added. "I'm excited about becoming a teacher, but I was a little bit disappointed when I thought that I wouldn't have real clients."

"I'm really happy for you, Gren."

Gren walked one last time around the small dwelling. She couldn't believe that she was about to leave it forever. So, much had happened there. The place was filled with great memories, and some memories that were not so great. "Maybe I should just stay here," she said. "Ladinda told me that living in the Teachers' Building is optional."

"You can't stay here, Gren," Lawson told her. It took everything in him to say those words.

"Why not?"

"Because it's a two unit trip! Each way! You're a lot more practical than that."

Gren sighed. "I know. I'm just..."

"Me too."

Gren took one final look back before closing the door behind her for the final time. She and Lawson then walked down to her glidemobile, hand in hand. "I'm glad that I already had a chance to say goodbye to Sham and Titus," Gren commented. "They're both like family, but I want my final few micros here to be spent only with you." She wiped away a tear.

"Hey, don't say it like that!" Lawson was trying hard to be strong, but he felt like he was going to start crying himself at any micro. "We'll still see each other all the time. As soon as I get my first new paycheck from Haas, I plan to buy my own glidemobile. Then it's only a unit drive each if we meet in the middle. We can get together each rotation for the evening meal. There are plenty of good restaurants that we should try, or we can picnic somewhere. We'll spend so much time together that we'll feel like nothing has changed."

Gren managed a weak smile. "Haas isn't paying you that well, and I'm making a lot less."

"Okay, maybe every other rotation. And I do intend to buy a glidemobile right away."

Gren was silent for several micros. She couldn't remember the last time that she and Lawson had gone more than a couple of rotations without seeing each other. They had been partners at the Learning Center as young children, and had been inseparable ever since. "I don't know if I can do it," she said at last.

"You're the strongest person that I know," Lawson said sincerely. "Of course you can do it. Your teaching this class will revolutionize the next generation of Wanderers. How many times has being able to wander distances saved us? It's unexplored territory for so many practices, even Haas doesn't know how to do it! Think of it this way. If more people knew how to wander distances, maybe Ryker and Eli would have been rescued a lot sooner."

"Ryker and Eli had farium oxitate in their systems so no one would have been able to find them," Gren reminded him.

"Not originally," Lawson said. "A rescue team might have been able to locate them before they ever had to eat any of those disgusting plants."

"Good point."

"You've always wanted to make a difference, Gren. This job is giving you the opportunity to do just that."

"But I've never been on my own before. I've always had you. And lately, I've also had Sham and Titus. Calli and Tayo to some extent as well."

Lawson laughed. "Sham is trying hard to figure out where Calli can stay when she comes to visit him, since you won't be here anymore."

"That's Sham, always so unselfish." Gren smiled. "I hope Calli knows what she's getting into."

Lawson was happy to see Gren smile. "Probably not. Listen, as much as I hate to say it, you need to get going. You've got a long trip ahead of you, and you'll want to unpack and get settled in as soon as you arrive."

"You're right." Gren opened the door of the glidemobile but didn't get in. "Lawson, there's one thing that I need to tell you before I go."

"What's that?"

Gren looked deep into Lawson's eyes. "I love you. I always have." She moved even closer and they shared their second kiss ever.

"I love you too."

Gren got into her glidemobile, started it, and after one glance back, drove away.

Lawson stood outside of Gren's former building for several micros after the vehicle was out of sight. It felt good to have finally said the words that he had kept bottled up inside of him for so long. It felt even better to have heard Gren say the same thing to him. He tried to blink back a few tears, but instead they started to flow freely. He missed her already.

Epilogue

As the ride slowed down Gren realized that she and Lawson were holding hands. It felt natural. Their relationship had always been only friendship and a mild flirtation. They had hinted at maybe having something more sometime in the future, but they both had so much going on that they agreed that the timing wasn't right for a romance.

Gren glanced at the others in the Test Track car with them. The teenage boy was putting his hat back on. The young girl behind them had a huge smile on her face. "That was fun, Mommy!" she said loudly. "I loved going so fast at the end!" The girl who looked like Calli had her head turned. Gren couldn't see her face.

"Let's try to catch up to her when we get off," Lawson whispered. He also noticed that he was holding hands with Gren, but didn't do anything about it. Her hand felt right in his. "We could just ask her how she liked the ride."

"Okay."

As Gren and Lawson got off they thought that the young woman would try to disappear again, but instead she approached them. "That was unexpected, wasn't it?"

"Who are you?" Lawson asked.

"I could ask you the same thing." She paused. "My name's Calli, but you and Gren already know that. Before you ask, it's short for Callisto, which is one of the moons of Jupiter. My dad's an amateur astronomer. And it could have been worse, I could have been named Ganymede. Hey, let's get something to eat. I'm starving. We can then talk and maybe figure some of this out. How about Electric Umbrella? I'd love a Veggie Flatbread. I know it's early, but they should be open by now, and I skipped breakfast this morning."

Gren had a million questions, but it was obvious that Calli didn't want to talk until they were inside the restaurant. They all ordered their meals and then headed up the stairs. It would be quieter up there. They took a table that was far away from all of the other guests.

"So, what's going on?" Calli asked immediately.

"That's what I was about to ask you," Lawson said.

"I have no idea. All I know is that sometimes strange things happen when I'm here. It's always been on Rock 'n' Roller Coaster before, and I had to have a special paper FASTPASS with me."

"Was it given to you by Roy?" Gren asked.

"Yes! How did you know?"

"The same thing happened to us," Lawson replied.

Gren reached into her pocket and pulled out the pressed penny. "What about these?" she asked. "Did these pennies have something to do with what just happened?"

"I don't know," Calli said. "It was the strangest thing. A cast member handed them to me earlier. He told me to keep one and to give the other two away. He said that I would know who to give them to. Now that I think about it, the cast member's name was 'Ward'."

"Sounds familiar," Lawson mumbled.

"I didn't even realize that I had dropped them until you tried to give one of them back to me," Calli continued. "And somehow I knew that you needed to hang onto them. I'm really glad that I ran into you two, I thought I was going crazy. Actually, I had decided that the previous two times had been dreams. You guys are lucky, you get to go through it together. I haven't had anyone to turn to, until now."

"I have another question," Lawson said. "When we saw you earlier, you took off. Why?"

"I was a little bit freaked out," Calli explained. "As I said, I thought that the whole thing before was a dream or that I was crazy. When I saw the two of you, I was pretty sure that it was the latter."

"I can understand that," Gren said. "Last year my little sister rode with us, and she's since decided that she dreamed it."

"Winnie rode too?" Calli asked. Gren nodded. "I can understand why she would want to forget that one! It's kind of strange, here I just met you and I already know the name of your sister. I wonder if that means that Sham is real. He's really cute."

"But just because something happened over there doesn't mean that it is real over here," Gren pointed out.

"Yeah, but sometimes it is," Calli said. "I mean, look at the two of you. You're now dating in both places." She noticed the look that her new friends gave each other. "I'm sorry, I guess I just jumped to conclusions."

Gren was obviously embarrassed, so Lawson decided to try to explain. "I guess we're kind of like the 'us' on the ride, at least how they were. We're the best of friends and we know that the timing isn't right for anything more." He decided to change the subject. "At least the part about your broken ankle isn't true."

Calli laughed. "Actually, it is. I broke it a couple of months ago. I just finished up physical therapy last week. That's why I walked fast when you saw me, running is still hard. I plan to have it back in shape by January, though, so I can run in the marathon."

"The marathon?" Lawson repeated. "Are you here a lot, or are you local?"

"Born and raised in Kissimmee," Calli answered. "I'm definitely a Florida girl, I've never even seen snow."

"You haven't missed anything," Gren replied. "I'm from Massachusetts, but I live here now."

"I'm local as well," Lawson replied. "Hey, maybe we can all hangout again sometime. It would be fun to compare notes on what happened the other times."

"That sounds like a great idea!" Calli handed Lawson her phone. "Here, add your number and then I'll text you mine. You too, Gren."

"Um..." Gren said slowly.

Lawson didn't notice. He took the phone from Calli. "We're here a lot," he said. He typed in his number and handed the phone to Gren, but she didn't do anything with it. "It's a good thing that our real story isn't like the one that we just experienced, with Gren moving away."

"Um, Lawson?" Gren said. "There's something that I need to tell you."

"What?"

"My internship? They're moving me to the Jacksonville office."

Calli immediately felt like she was intruding. "I'm going to run to the bathroom. I'll be right back." She took her phone from Gren and walked away.

Lawson waited until Calli was out of sight before saying anything else. "What?"

"I just found out this morning. My boss called me right before I left for the park. It came out of the blue, I had no idea that it might happen."

"When?"

Gren sighed. "I leave at the end of next month. I'm going to have to find someone to sublet my apartment, plus I have to pack everything up. It's going to be a crazy few weeks."

"Is it a permanent move?" was Lawson's next question.

"I don't know. I'm hoping that they'll offer me a full time position after my internship is over, and maybe that would be back at the office here."

"Jacksonville is so far away," Lawson complained.

"It's only a couple of hours! I'll be back all the time, and we'll still have our park days. We just won't be able to get together as often during the week." She placed her hand on top of Lawson's. "Your friendship is more important to me than any internship or potential job. We'll be closer than ever."

Lawson's phone went off and he looked down at it. "It's Calli. She wants to know if we need more time to talk."

"That's up to you."

Lawson looked into Gren's eyes. "Promise we'll make it work?"

Gren nodded. "I promise."

"Okay, let me text her back."

A few moments later Calli rejoined her new friends.

"Everything okay?"

"Yeah, it will be," Lawson replied.

"Good." Calli handed Gren her phone. "I still need your number, you didn't add it before." Gren typed it in and gave the phone back to Calli. "I need to get going. I'm looking for an apartment, and I promised myself that I would spend the afternoon online."

"I'm going to be subletting my place," Gren said. "It's small, but it's in a safe area, and the rent is reasonable. It's also furnished."

"Just like the other Gren's dwelling," Calli pointed out. "Maybe we can set something up? I still need to go, though, so I'll text you."

"Sounds good."

Calli gave hugs to both Gren and Lawson. "I know we just met, but I feel like I've known you forever."

"I know what you mean," Lawson replied.

After Calli left, Gren and Lawson stayed at the table for half an hour. Having met someone from that other place, they couldn't help but wonder who else they might run into. Lawson was also trying to let the idea that Gren was leaving sink in.

They spent the entire day at the park. At the end of the evening they found a good spot to watch IllumiNations. Lawson put his arm around Gren during the show and she didn't seem to mind. At one point Gren rested her head on Lawson's shoulder. They could both sense that their relationship was about to change.

After the last firework they held back and let the crowd disperse a bit before leaving themselves. Neither of them felt the need to rush out. Since Gren was parked in a close parking lot Lawson walked her to her car. It made more sense to walk than to take the tram. Lawson owned a motorcycle, and it wasn't parked far away. "This day was certainly unexpected," Gren commented as she took out her keys.

Lawson nodded. "Can I ask you something?"

"Anything."

"Have you ever thought about being more than friends?"

Gren looked away. "Yeah. But it scares me. I've known people who started as friends and when they broke up they hated each other. Your friendship is the most important thing in my life, and I don't want to lose it."

"I've known people like that as well," Lawson said. "But I also know some couples who are incredibly strong because they have the basis of a solid friendship."

"My parents were like that," Gren admitted. "They met in college, but they didn't start dating until after they had both graduated."

"I don't want to lose you, Gren. I thought that we had time, but since you're moving maybe we don't. If you're not ready, don't worry, I won't be hurt. Just like the other Lawson said, I want you in my life, no matter what."

"I want you in my life as well."

"We don't have to make any decisions tonight," Lawson continued. "And if you want to stay only friends I can live with that. You're the best friend that I've ever had, and if changing our relationship is going to hurt who we are, then I don't want it to change."

"Nothing is going to hurt who we are," Gren said. "I won't let it."

"Good." Lawson took Gren's hand and kissed it. "Good night, my dear friend. I'll talk to you tomorrow." They shared a hug, then Gren got into her car.

Lawson walked slowly to his motorcycle, purposely not looking back. He couldn't believe that Gren was moving. Just like the other Lawson, he missed her already.

A Mouse Gate Adventure Book
What's your adventure?

www.mousegate.com

Title: *DreamWanderers-Escape*
- Author: Paula Brown
- Publisher: Mouse Gate Press
- Paper Back: ISBN: 9781590957912
- eBook: ISBN: 9781590958766
- Number of pages 240
- Publication Date: August 16, 2016

Dream Wanderers guide you through your worst nightmares. Far across the universe, an elite school runs a special program, training the Dream Wanderers of tomorrow.

But what happens when…

Gren and Lawson will soon achieve the impossible, becoming the first male/female partners to make it through the program. Or will they? Their feelings for each other and Lawson's disdain for an unbreakable rule, risk their expulsion.

They wander into a nightmare of their own…

When Lawson and Gren disappear, most assume they've run away together. But their four best friends aren't so sure. Following a shaky clue, they enlist the help of a crazy old man and set out to find the truth. Soon, the dream Wanderers will take on an entire army, as the fate of two worlds hangs in the balance.

Title: *Dream Wanderers Apprentices*
- Author: Paula Brown
- Publisher: Mouse Gate Press
- Paper Back: ISBN: 9781590957929
- eBook: ISBN: 9781590957936
- Number of pages 240
- Publication Date: August 16, 2016

A visit from Gren's little sister and a friend turns dangerous because of a case of mistaken identity; and it is up to Gren and her friends to use their talents and find the girl before it's too late.

Gren is excited because her little sister Winnie and Winnie's friend Mollie are going to spend their school break with her. Gren's friends Calli and Tayo agree to spend their break with her as well, to help take care of the children while Gren is at work. What Gren doesn't know is that Mollie has a problem that she wants assistance with; her dreams come true. Someone learns of Mollie's ability to see the future and sets a plan in motion to kidnap her and profit from her gift. What the person doesn't realize is that Winnie was grabbed instead. Gren and her friends use their skills to try to find Winnie, before the kidnapper realizes the mistake.

Title: *Dream Wanderers Trials*
- Author: Paula Brown
- Publisher: Mouse Gate Press
- Paper Back: ISBN: 9781590950166
- eBook: ISBN: 9781590950180
- Number of pages 248
- Publication Date: March 5, 2019

They sat back because the ride had started. Gren could not stop thinking about the young woman seated behind them. The news that she had to share with Lawson also weighed heavily on her mind. Her favorite part of the ride was the end, when it looked like they were about to hit a wall but instead the car went outside and sped up to 65MPH. Gren sat back to enjoy it. As they neared the fake wall, everything started to blur.

www.ingramcontent.com/pod-product-compliance
Lightning Source LLC
Chambersburg PA
CBHW061611100726
47898CB00002B/608